Incomplete Love Stories

Heart touching tales behind the curtains of time

PRAMOD PRAKASH PATIL

© **Pramod Prakash Patil 2019**

All rights reserved

All rights reserved by author. No part of this publication may be reproduced, stored in a retrieval system or transmitted in any form or by any means, electronic, mechanical, photocopying, recording or otherwise, without the prior permission of the author.

Although every precaution has been taken to verify the accuracy of the information contained herein, the author and publisher assume no responsibility for any errors or omissions. No liability is assumed for damages that may result from the use of information contained within.

First Published in April 2019

ISBN: 978-93-5347-401-0

BLUE ROSE PUBLISHERS

www.bluerosepublishers.com

info@bluerosepublishers.com

+91 8882 898 898

Cover Design:
Deepak Lal

Typographic Design:
Teena Maurya

Distributed by: Blue Rose, Amazon, Flipkart, Shopclues

Dedicated to

The skilful gardener of my life, who made me, educated me and taught me to live life with struggles and filled my heart with love for literature and knowledge, my grandmother late Smt. Dwarika N. Patil, I dedicate my first flower to her remembrance. If she would not have in my life then it was impossible for me to take education. This is my dream work which is inspired by so many people who has their own incomplete love story. I dedicate my work to them who inspired me to bring their story into the focus. I also dedicate my work to my parents and my village who always inspired me and stood behind me.

Acknowledgement

It's very incredible moment for me to bring this my first novel in your hands. No doubt that writing a book is hard work but without some inspiration it is not possible. It was so difficult to complete this book without moral, emotional and economical support of my mother Mrs. Vaishali P. Patil , my father Shri. Prakash N. Patil and my wife Dipika Patil, without their support I could not possible to write this book. I am very thankful them to understand me and nurtured my writing skills. Thanks to my dear brother Shri. Ganesh P. Patil. Who helped many times regarding typing and contain formatting, it was difficult to bring it without his help. Without my friends, Vishal Jain, Rahul Patil, Rohit Patil and Arif Pinjari, Kanhaiyyalal Patil and other my dear friends it was not possible to get the idea about the book, thanks to them who always stood behind me in my support. They in fact realised me that I can write something productive. Special thanks to Mrs. Sheetal P. Satare who motivated and inspired me to bring my idea and imagination into reality on the paper and did all assistance regarding financial support and contains formatting. it was not possible without her support.

I am very thankful to Pro. Arvind P. Joshi, Pro. Dipak Chaudhary, Pro Suresh Agle Pro. G. D. Sapkal and all my teachers DES College of Education, Dhule (MS) and SSVPS Arts & Com College, Dhule, where

I studied about literature and got inspired from their beautiful lectures. They gave me the real guidance about the literature and helped me to express my ideas and imaginations through the words.

Impact of my village, its traditions and customs made me; I grew by watching them and learnt many things of life. Life is not simple and always has many turns and diversion, thanks to my village where I enriched my writing skills. I saw many ups and downs during that period, thanks to Mr. Rajendra Marathe and Mahesh Pawar as well as Shree Bajaj Computers and Shivam Foundation, Sunrise Vidyalaya, Dindoli, Surat, who supported me morally and mentally.

Special thanks to Bluerose Publishers and the Team who gave me chance to reach you, without their assistance it can't be possible to publish the book.

Heartily thanks to all my relatives and to them who helped me directly and indirectly I would like to remain always in their debts.

Always in your gratitude

— Pramod P Patil

Preface

First I want to say you thank to show your interest in this my dream book. As we know that man is the social animal and he likes to live in society. He can't live without society. This society affects on his living and behaviours in many ways. Man himself made society, its traditions and customs as well as some rules and regulations for its existence. But most of the times the same things are responsible to change our own life. There are many things which we can't define in words but just we can feel by heart and with emotions. 'Love' is the same word which is unable to explain because the definition of the word is always variable to everyone.

Through this book I don't want to hurt anyone's personal life and his feeling but just tried to explore the way we love to someone in our life. There is always first love in every one's life and these stories are the respectful salute them who did loyal and pure love which is alive in their deep of the heart till the moment. Many are succeeded to get it but every heart has one 'incomplete love story'. It's just searching for their loved one. I hope these stories will recall your love and makes happy what you have today.

What we need to live, Food, shelter, clothes etc.? Sure. But most important is love. I don't want to make any difference in love. It doesn't mean that love is only related to girl or boy. It's a universal concept. We always love to our family members, relatives, friends and such many. But sometimes we fall in love with someone who is not belonging to our caste, blood and race. Just we attach our feelings and emotions with the person.

My target is not to show it is wrong or right but to do it with great respect and loyalty. When we start to love someone we simply forget everything which is natural, no doubt. But don't try to deceive any one or try to use anyone for lust or any other profit and also one shouldn't fall down to destroy oneself in any blind love. These all things should think by young generations. Modern generation have their own conceptions about the love, in fact they must have their own but their concept shouldn't humiliate our culture. I just want to show the mirror for the way we love to someone. I hope it will be the guideline for them. Love is always there, only we should dare to get it. I know when we love to someone he or she is gold for us but it is our duty to check it out into the furnace, it is possible that it would be copper or iron what we were considered as gold.

We are always blind in love and so we can't see many things around our flower. In fact love is like wooden block; throw it into the sea, if you really love it. And if it will come back to you then be sure that it is your true love but that time you have has such dignity to accept your love one and if it will never come then supposed it was not yours. You must believe in yourself. Suicide is not only the way to leave all these.

When somebody left you then there can be two reasons. Either you are not liable for him/her or she/he was not liable for you. Love is the beginning of life with or our mother's love, and I don't think that anyone will love you more than her. There is no any comparison with her love. Our love has gone means everything is lost; this idea is not the thread of good life. There are many things to do except love in the world. Real love never makes you waste. You should not say 'I am falling in love' but you must say 'I am rising in love'.

It will help you complete your love story.

Disclaimer

I hereby declare that some stories are inspired by real lives in my life but it doesn't mean that I presented them all as it was happened with them. I managed them according to my imagination. Remaining stories are inspired only by pure imagination. There is no any relation between these stories and anyone's personal life. If anyone found any relation with them, it supposed only coincident. This fiction is published to entertain reader and they should take as only amusement. There is no personal hatred about anyone.

Contents

Acknowledgement v

Preface vii

1. Was It Just Attraction? 1

2. "Love: Can be also like this!" 15

3. Unfortunate Love 30

4. Small Mistake 40

5. Othello Revised 53

6. Love Is Friend, Philosopher And Guide! 65

7. I Am Sorry…. 87

8. Slap 97

9. Waiting for love 111

10. Thread 126

1

Was It Just Attraction?

"Oh my dear baby, see what is there. Water, water, do you want water!! No. what my dear baby wants ………." One mother was trying to make her son silent but why he was crying, nobody knew.

"Are you mad Sonia? Make him silent quick. You are mother and you should know all the tricks to make him silent." The man said to his wife.

"Then why don't you try for this Mr.? You are also father. You should also use some tricks ….."

Husband and wife both started safe quarrel but originally it was not dispute. One cannot take seriously that both were piping into their heart.

Prem was looking the scene very carefully may be some answers were hidden in their words. He was going to his village from Pune by train. He just stood to the door wanted to throw out him from the train, going to commit suicide. Prem started to journey from Pune to Jalgaon at that night. Might he have decided that it was last journey of his life? It was platform no. 1 which made him mad and inspired to make serious crime. He decided to throw out himself out of the train at the time of dark but who knows the games of fate. Tearful eyes, absent mind and unconscious brain can do anything.

Prem, a young boy, just completed his post graduation from university, and was searching the job for better settlement of life. Family conditions were not as satisfied as any common man expects still it was not so bad. Brilliant student of the college completed his education on his own strengths. So in that he had to do many types of jobs on the private level. Even sometimes in hotels or nightclubs or tuition or in computer classes etc. It's a reality that there are many ways to earn the money for the person who keeps himself ready for any work. And doing all the jobs targeted only towards the completing the education. It was his final goal. Surely he knew that once he complete the education will never do such hazardous efforts to settle the life. It was education, which made him confident about the future. At least he was expected this by getting good job. But nobody knows about the dark future. Nobody can say what is in the hands of time for that we closely waiting, it always ruptures the planes and future and having great shifting and spoils

Prem was started to work in a private computer class for part time job. Due to this many students came into his contacts but most of the time he tried to keep a safe distance with them and especially with the girl students. On the same time a girl had taken an admission for the course. She was quite naughty, beautiful, intelligent and self confident. Actually Prem was not a guy who can fall in love with any type of girl but he didn't know about him what would come in his way. Hence, he could remain single even in his last year of the college.

She was taking an education in another city; here she came at her uncle's house to spend her summer vacation for four months. So she decided to take some knowledge of the computer within that useful time. Prem saw this girl first time and fall in love with this girl, her name was Ashwini. But he didn't know that one day his life will keep only 'ash' after this name.

He was only looking towards her and observing for one hour and even forgot that many students were catching him at. He thought many times to express his love for her but dared not to tell that he love her. In fact how could he do this while everywhere we want an experience? On the other side Ashwini was also quite attracted with the name 'Prem'. And most important was his behaviour and well nature. She started to discuss many things with him and wanted to know more about him. Even she came to know in few why Prem was looking at him. But how can it possible that one girl will say about her love to the boy. Generally we have the concept about this that boy should express his love. Prem was different type of boy who believed in the spiritual love. Finally Ashwini came to know that the boy will never express his love. Actually she also likes him so much but she doesn't know why?

One day Prem was seating in his class. Suddenly

his mobile rang and the voice made him aware. Yes, it was Ashwini.

"Hello sir, what are you doing?"

"Nothing, just i am waiting here for my friend." He replied.

"Sir, if you have time, I want to tell you one important thing."

"Sure. You can tell. Is there any problem?"

"I fell in love with one boy. And I like him very much." She gave an information to him as she wanted to fired him and the words were started work out. With these words Prem turn into cold.

"What has happened sir? You will not ask me who the boy is?" she asked in teasing mood.

He cut the call and switch off the phone without asking her who did she loves. Next day Ashwini came to him and told him, "Sir, I know you are looking towards me each time but why are you so shy to propose. Sir I love you and I like you. I know you will not say this one. Bye. I am waiting for your answer." She proposed him directly; it was unexpected shock for the Prem. He felt that it was the happiest moment of his life. Something he got what he was searching. He was completely shocked and impressed about her daring to propose him. Now his love became double for her. From that day both started to chat on mobile at night, sometime midnight of sometime full night they were started. Simply when you get something good and glittering, have to pay something for that.

Brilliant student slowly took out himself out of the study unknowingly. Whole of his concentration he started to focus in the making of dream of love with

Ashwini. Suddenly all the nights were turned into pinks while it is dark for the others. Definitely all things were new and unknown for the Prem such like love, beloved, her gift etc. and first their meeting in Swaminarayan temple was surely fantastic for him. For this meeting he went on riding bicycle more than seven kilometres. What was happening he didn't know but something was enormous happening for him?

They both didn't understand how four months were passed away and the time came to be separated when she had to move back to her home for her school. Actually one can be happy while go back to the home with the heart of love. But their love reached beyond the limitations. They would be in contact but who knew that how much their heart will remember each other.

Here Prem was always in her memory and always thinking about her love, beauty and n the other hand Ashwini concentrated herself on her study and engaged with new friends. She told Prem to focus on his study while he called her anytime. They both believe on each other that no one can break their love while they forgot that one of the can do this unfortunate thing.

They were talking all the things what they could talk. Such like love, marriage, life and so on. For that we say 'love is blind' and can never see the reality of the life. Prem forgot the reality of his life. He forgot the conditions of his life.

They both were started new game of the life or we can say started new chapter of life. Ashwini was quite practical girl so she used to behave practically with the Prem. But on the other hand Prem was quite emotional one who blindly sank in the love. Time and future always ready to destroy yours plans.

Prem shocked one day when he called to Ashwini.

"Hello, Ashwini is their?"

"Yes. Who are you?" she replied and asked unexpected question to him. Still he dared to say her

"It's me, my dear, Prem, your love."

"Shut up Prem. is it the language to talk with anyone? How stupid you are!!!"She taught him.

"And by the way, what I told you. Don't call me without getting receives my call." She opens her anger.

'But Ashu you didn't call me from last three months. So I called you. I love you Ashu. And I can't live without you." He tried to set her anger cool down but she was fired more as if he thrown rock oil in the fire.

"O listen mad boy. Before that you were not dead or will not after that. Just remember don't try to call me again till I will make the call." She ordered him and cut the call.

Here poor boy was confused that what was happened and what mistake ha had made. Why she said like this? Such many questions were coming in his mind and brain was unable to answer them. And he got complete effect on his university examinations. Those things were happened, which were not expected even to anyone. Simply he neglected towards the exam and gave paper for only as formality he completed. Therefore his result made everyone confused. But when he understood about his result, time had played its game. He was completely fell down from the expectations of his friends, teachers and family members. No friends were in his support but how they bear that their one friend on whom they proud so much, was came down very in final exam.

There were many things to entertain to Prem but he never looked at anyone for moment. It was so easy for him to make any affair with any girl in the college. He was not only a talent student of the college but also a good actor, poet, debater, anchor, speaker and always active in various activities of the college. So it was so simple for him to fall in love more than one time. He believed on the spirituality of the love, often he thought that his beloved should be his wife, that was Ashwini and therefore he dint want to deceive her on any price.

His very few friends were known about his love story. One his best Rahul asked him about Ashwini on the occasion of teacher's day celebration. It was his second year of post graduation. He become so much nervous when Rahul asked him a simple question'

"Prem, how is our Bhabhi, means your Ashwini? You will not tell to us. Are you in contact or not with her?" Prem smiled with natural shy but answered them that she was fine and he called her before many days. Now many times he tried but she didn't receive his calls. Actually he wanted to congratulate her. She stood first in final exams in her college.

"Prem I am observing you from many days. Is there any problem at home? If it is please tell. Don't forget that your friend is alive."

"No. Nothing at all, Rahul. Everything is fine at home. I am worried about only exams." Prem replied.

"Ok. But remember regular contact can only make any relation strong... ok let me go. My friends are waiting in the canteen. We will meet tomorrow. Bye" said Rahul in the sense of great philosopher. Prem smiled and turned towards gymkhana of the college. Words of Rahul made big blast in his brain and the mind, as if both started rebel for love and freedom. He started thinking more on the words taught by the Rahul. Suddenly he came to understand that seven month had passed for last words with Ashwini. And still today he was waiting for her call. Really was it matter of regular contact. But he refused the words of Rahul by saying himself "no my Ashwini is not like this. She can't live without me. We love each other how much no one had done it before us. We will prove it and sure will settle an instance for the people who think negatively about it." Said this and many things, often he was saying himself regularly.

He felt that she was always with him, saying 'love you Prem' when Prof. Pawar was teaching them famous drama of William Shakespeare,' Romeo and Juliet'. All students were focused on the board but except Prem. He was completely drowned in the dream as if Shakespeare had written this drama only for him. His blind love Ashwini made him a Romeo and threw all the things away from. There was girl Pooja in his class who liked Prem heartily. She had never expressed her love for Prem to anywhere. Actually she was good friend of Prem. Whenever he felt need about exam, study or any other difficulty, he never worried about it. Because the name was always ready to aid him 'Pooja'. But unfortunately she couldn't tell her love for Prem, even to her best friend Shalini. Really gives some special things to some special people, same there was Shalini. Indirectly she came to know something about them both. It's generally said that one boy and girl can't be only friends always. Shalini decided to open out the reality between their relations. While many times she forced Pooja to tell all the things between them. But what could she said about it when she wasn't sure about Prem. finally Pooja accepted her love for Prem. Now Shalini was waiting for the chance to tell the thing to Prem.

And one day Shalini decided to ask Prem what was he thinking about Pooja when she saw him seating alone in the college garden. "Hii Prem. I want to talk with you something if you don't have time."

"What Shalini? I have always time for my friends. Tell what do want to ask?" he replied.

"And what is about Pooja? You don't have time for her. Who is for you, dude" she asked.

"What do mean, Shalini? I can't understand, what are you asking? Off course she is my good friend"

"But she doesn't think this only, Mr. Prem. She has something different for you my dear friend. Can't you see something in her eyes for you? She loves you Prem. How cant you feel it?"

"Sorry Shalini. But you have some misunderstanding about our friendship. She can't do this. I know she is good girl. And I can't think such things for her anyhow. And who is this mad told you such mad think."

"She is only mad who told me about her love for you, Prem. Who should have told me this? And tell me why she should not? And good girl can't love to anyone? Or she is not human."

Prem got shocked when listen that thing. But more than that question came in his mind that what answer he should give to her? Shalini was still standing in front of him. He came to know that it was the good time tells all the things to Shalini id didn't want to face the Pooja.

"Shalini, I really don't know about her mind. I'm really sorry for that. But I can't do this with her.

Because I love someone else....someone is already in my life. Ashwini!!"

Shalini was shocked to listen this thing because no anyone can thinks about this boy can also be in love. He told everything to Shalini.

"But Prem, still I request you dear don't deny her love. From last five years she is in love Prem. As a friend I can give you advice. But I want to tell you one thing. I don't know about your Ashwini but remember Pooja will be the best for because you know about Ashwini but Pooja know you well. After all, the decision is yours." she said him finally.

He answered her, "Sorry Shalini I can't deceive to my love. What she will do I don't know but I will be always with her. But want to request you as good friend please convince Pooja to forget about me. And take care of her. I fear that she will do something wrong with herself."

"You don't worry about it, Prem. I know her very well. She will not do such mad thing. Instead I pray to God that something should not happen wrong with you Prem. I hope you will get everything what you expect." she left him alone there without expecting any answer and started walk towards library. He was looking her far going image.

After that Prem never wanted or dared to talk with Pooja or even with Shalini. Meanwhile he noticed that Ashwini didn't want to talk with him. She started to ignored him. After long he called her. Within that short conversation he came to know about her education. She had taken an admission for M.Tech. In wel reputed college in Pune. But this time he wasn't as happy as he expected because his dearest one haven't shared this most important thing with him. He was upset due to her such negligent conduct for him. His mind was thinking about her conduct, many questions were killing him that 'why she didn't tell him even about her good achievement. Didn't she feel need to talk with me about?' but after all he was so blind in her love. Finally his blind love concluded the topic that she was doing all the things for their love only. Now, he could not stop himself to meet her.

Somehow he had completed his post graduation but unfortunately he could not find any good job, after his PG up to six months. Meanwhile he did small and invaluable work, left that he did nothing. Nobody can accept such child who is not earning money till after his 24 years of age. Parents were also disturbed. All were started giving him advice about job in Pune or Mumbai. Now he got chance to go at Pune for job when his parents advised him. He had an idea that he could do the job where his love one was waiting for him. Now who will not accept the great opportunity to do the both works together? Nobody can explain the delight he got with this great idea. He wanted to give her surprise that he was there hence he didn't contact her before leaving. He was so much happy with such imagination that how she will be surprise on unknown moment. How she would be react with his presence. That great thinking was making him romantic.

Early in the morning Ashwini got the message on her mobile, "Good morning Ashu!!"She was surprised about unknown number and replied, "Good morning. But who are you?" But the next message stretched her eyebrow with tension and hatred. "I am your love, Prem. I am in Pune. Dear I want to meet you. If you allow for and having free time." Unknowingly she gave a message with time as if an appointment.

Here Prem got message and became so much happy dreaming her meeting. He reached in her college before 30 minutes and waits the same time. He was completely sunk in her image that was seemed before five years. He could only imagine her how she was looking then. Anybody can imagine that the time of waiting is so much hard. He was feeling of passing thirty years within those 30 minutes. Within those thirty minutes he recalled her all memories that both had passed. He was totally confused about their discursion what to talk with her and how he would be faced her. He was still preparing himself to face her.

Finally the moment came for what he was waiting from five years. What a long period it is for someone. He saw her after a long period of five years completely. One can noticed that it was not a short period. Naturally one can think to hug to our love one; nothing has wrong about Prem when he thought about this. But he got surprised when she kept safe distance from Prem. As soon as she came in front of him she asked simple question. "Tell fast, what do you want to say? And do you come here?" Now Prem was surely confused with her questions. Because he till that moment he didn't know what really he wanted. He thought might be she was tired with study or her mood is so sad or she is not unhappy with him. So he started his good and lovely words with her. He could not understand her behaviour when she was only delivering verbal responses to him, most of them were not positive. Suddenly after few time when she got tired, said, "Prem please stop this nonsense. You don't have something new to talk. I understand your love but sorry I don't love you." He was only looking her face. What to say now. Initially he thought she was making joke about it but on the next moment he sobered.

"I know I made a mistake. Actually, it was childish game when I told you about love. I was unknown about my life and career. Now I'm mature to understand the things. I think you should have also forgotten such mad things. Now I understood that 'It was just an attraction.' It was not love."

"But Ashu I really love. Why did you do this with me then? I was happy with my life. You taught me this. You shown me the rout of this love and you are telling me to forget it. I you are joking this. Ashu please stop it if it is a joke, it's hurting me."

"No Prem it's not joke. Just I am showing the reality that you don't want to see. I am sorry for if you are hurting. I don't want to keep you in the dark. "

"But Ashu what are doing from seven years? You told me that you could not live without me. You promised me and gave many reasons why do you love me, were these all fake?"

"Prem I can't understand, how can well educated guy like you believe on such foolish things? And ok it just coincident to propose you. What is something special in you to love? And one thing remembers no any girl can love you. Nobody likes such foolish guy, Prem, who can't understand the desires of any girl. Simply I used you for my classes. Later on I really wanted physical relationship with you but you made angry about you concept of spiritual love, marriage etc. mad things. Finely I came to know that you can't do anything. And please now listen. Don't come in front of me if you want to live in Pune. You don't have any background of good family. And see you are jobless, how can I love you? How can about marriage? And please don't come in my college campus again. If you really love me, let me go. By the way my boy friend is waiting for me. Take care. Bye!" she left but still he was looking at her.

Large whistle brought him in real world. He settled his attention on the couple trying to make their child silent. Suddenly his mother's face came in front of him, tried each time relax him, his father who could do anything for him. They were loving to him so much and recalling their love makes his full of tears. The words told by his ex beloved 'it was just attraction' started spinning in his brain. Is the love of my parents and this couple for their child attraction? He got the answer 'no'. But he was unsure about his love. Dead blind love brought him into the conscious. And his conscious mind said, "Prem don't try to stop your life. Live for them who really love you. Don't die for them who gave you this precious life. " now he understood why the first love is unforgettable. First time felt the existence of tear and pleasure together.

At the time of midnight Ashwini got the message "sorry Ashwini, you are wrong. It was not an attraction. It is a pure love. You are failed to understand it dear. And don't worry I will not come back in your life. However Pune is far away. And thanks for shown me the reality. I am happy but problem is that now I can't love to anyone because I can't forget you. Good bye. Take care." She could not take sleep for whole night.

***

2

"Love: Can be also like this!"

"Hello", Vishal received the call and trying to know what the person wanted to tell. Whole house is full of crowd. Complete house had taken the form of market. Arrival of the guests was started from the morning. Surely one can understand that there is the marriage function in the house. Vishal's father has fixed his marriage before days with nice looking girl, an only child of her father. And well educated girl lives in Pune. Still Vishal is not so much happy with all that is going to happened. From the morning Vishal started to receive the calls of friends and relatives. Mobile was completely busy in the call with the relatives, friends, business fellows, DJ fellow, and so on.

Decorator was getting himself busy in the arrangement of the decoration, how the decoration should be in the function. Many times he was asking to the Vishal about the arrangement and the decoration. But the mood of Vishal was completely got down. Finally he annoyed on the fellow and said, "Uncle Will you please do one thing? You please consult with my father about all the things."

"But, my son, it's your marriage and Bhau told me that all should be as your choice. He told me to ask you."

"Ok, I know what my father can say! But I will call you later. Don't mind uncle but in front of all relatives I can't talk with you how I want. And I am tired. So if you don't mind, we will discuss after some time. Let me be relaxed." He told with complete nervous mood to the fellow, trying to convince him but he could not tell him what was in his mind.

"Ok. I can understand about your headache. I know you came early in the morning and it difficult to work after the travel for whole night. You take rest; let me do my other works." The decorator told him as friend. "One thing, you will call or I should make you call"

'It will be better if you will do it." He laughs slightly and cut the call.

He glanced at the house and to all the people seating in the porch discussing about his marriage, how they tried to brought both families together. His father is also seating in the company of old people. How happy he was! Vishal was started thinking about his father. From the school time his father wasn't so much happy about his the average intelligent son. But now his father is so happy, unfortunately that happiness made Vishal unhappy and silent. 'How can a child taken out his joy who gave him all the things he needed and did everything for him. Not only this but also many reason, he remembered, his father was got satisfaction because of his any type of act. He saw his sisters with full of joy, making joke to all the relatives and friends. All had the smile of satisfaction and smile on their faces only because of Vishal. He was the youngest child in the family after his elder sisters and a big brother, whose marriage was the final marriage function in the family and they knew that they can't see such function for years now. That made them more energetic.

Suddenly, he got shocked came out from the thinking about the family. It was his mother asking for something. Might be she wanted to ask him whether he want something or not. She was mother and has care for the child always. Negatively he nodded his head though he didn't understand.

In such romantic and nice atmosphere Vishal was feeling alone and searching someone with complete disturb mind. He knew about one thing there were no one who could understand his mind and what was going on in his brain while there was big crowd of relatives and affectionate. Only one person could understand about him, he had an ability to read his eyes even. Suddenly words came on his lips that anyone could read easily, "where are you Pratham. I need of you bloody devil."

Pratham was his lovely and childhood friend where he could share his most of the problem and feel always safe. He said himself 'now this moment Pratham should have here, he can surely understand my problem and can make my confusion clear. Definitely if he would have seen my dull face, might have said "you stupid blind fellow, stop this madness. They are doing your marriage not putting you on hang. By the way if you don't like then I will marry with her, so smart your wife…..has" suddenly smile played hind and sick game on his lips. This thought made him laugh. What great magic of a real friend. Even his thought can also change the atmosphere and his presence gives confidence to fight with anyone. They has been living together many times such like watching cinema, eating panipuri, roaming out, and school , college also they remained together. They both knew each and every thing about each other and transmitting all tiny things to each other.

Today the whole family was ready in to the preparation of the marriage function, a beautiful and amazing moment of his life and how it was sad that his best friend was not with him. One can understand that how unfortunate it is when our most affectionate person doesn't attend the most memorable moment of our life.

Suddenly, his father noticed his unsatisfied eyes searching for something. It is so common for parent to get understand what is into the eyes of their children. His father was one of the respected people in the village. All people were calling 'Bhau' – a big brother. Always ready to help anyone therefore all were giving him respect. How could he neglect the nervous face of his lovely child? Finely he came to Vishal and asked "Vishal! What's happened beta? Aren't you feeling better? I think you should take the rest, you need it."

"No papa! You please don't think about such things. I'm better but just waiting for Pratham. Yes! I am tired but he will recover me and you know this better."

"Ohhh!! Then why don't you call him? Where

he is? I know you can't enjoy without him. Ok call him", his father said him in laughing moos as if saying about their friendship. Vishal also started laughing with his father. That simple words of his father made him quite relax, realized him that his father knows about his pain but how to show heart pain.

Within a moment, just he was thinking about his friend, group of ladies came to him and started teasing him with the lovely name of "bhabhiji" (his wife). All people started watching to the group that was started him teasing and sudden burst of laugh of the ladies around him attracted the focus of the group of boys, standing near at little distance. They all started laughing and started them watching as if hungry crane was staring towards the fishes in the pond. One of the naughty boys told him, "Bhaiya (brother) today you are so lucky. Enjoy the moment dude."

While girl told Vishal, "bhayya, take one laddoo please." That naughty boys said, "Give us also, we are so much hungry dear."

Suddenly girl got annoyed, "you stupid let me tell your sister, why you don't burn out there in hell. You are like donkey and honeybee, always roaming around us"

Now, Vishal got remember how he was making the fun in functions with his friends. He wanted to tell her that she was really like honey where these poor boys will go?' but controlled himself. Today he could not make any such objectionable comment. But he understood the indirect meaning of the girl that they are honey.

Vishal started to glance at the friend attended in his event. He was only looking at them and noticed about this all, perhaps he was thinking about his friend who could do more fun on the girls. Sweet smile came on his face when he remembers all the funs they made into the marriage ceremonies of their friends, how their dream girl was changing in each marriage ceremony. Each time Vishal would have to say that he had not seen such beautiful girl. All their friends were telling them in joke' you stupid came here for girls? This is our friend marriage. What will he think if he comes to know about your vagabond activities?" Actually everyone knew the answer but it was great fun to listen this funny thought of both.

"My friend our friend is going to marry and getting ready for the real pleasure of life. What should we do? Simple, we should also be ready for this turn. Who does know, when will god give us gift?" all starting laugh. "See how beautiful face it is! I am really searching such beautiful face." Vishal usually say these words in each ceremony.

Somebody makes him remember "Vishal last time also you said same words in Hershel's marriage." All starts laughing on the joke look to each other. But everyone knew that both of they had not dare to ask any girl, even their name also.

Ringtone of his mobile brought him in conscious from the old memories. It was Pratham, calling him. Suddenly his mood changed and became so happy but little annoyed on him due to his carelessness as if he became the child.

"Hello, you stupid fellow where are you? Can't you understand how I am feeling here without you? I am calling you mad since last two hours........." Vishal annoyed on him.

He started his questions without giving him a

chance to explain anything. Both were known about their behaviour for each other. Now Vishal came to understand what he was doing and said suddenly "Pratham sorry for that! But need you today most dear!"

Pratham felt that it was going wrong somewhere because till today such words had never come in their life. Now Pratham was on the anger "You stupid, how you can think that I am not with you? You fool I am waiting outside of the home, come out fast? And don't say sorry neither I will kill bloody fool."

Vishal knew about his friends how their manners and nature are. What to see then, Vishal stood up and ran fast towards the door and came out searching for his friend where his friend was waiting for him with sweet smile. He welcomed him in fact no need to welcome him .he was like the family member for Vishal and his family also known him very well. Their friendship was very famous in the village and there was no doubt for Pratham that Vishal wanted to tell him something that he could not share to anyone. Particularly both were known but still it was unclear about it.

"Tell me now stupid blind fellow, why are you so much anxious about my absence." Pratham said but Vishal didn't reply "by way, you have done nice arrangement of the function. See how all are happy and you? See your face in mirror; you are looking like stale potato"

"Yes. I know that everyone is happy and I am also trying to be happy dear but something is there which is unknown to you Pratham!"

"But your voice can't match with your word Vishal. You in our drama we have to be match both together. And you know one fine actor can do it perfectly.

But you are not an actor." Pratham told him in anger mood with strict watch in his eyes.

"Can we seat somewhere?" but both knew very well that they could not seat anywhere except their house. So they had to choose the place where nobody can disturb them without any strong reason.

"Pratham, her father called papa before five days yar, for his daughter's marriage with me!!" Vishal told him. "But you told me that her father had rejected uncle's proposal of the marriage. While uncle went them for Mayuri's hand for you" Pratham got confused.

"Yes I told you this when papa went to them. But what happened next, I was also unknown about it. Just yesterday I came to know." Vishal

"Ok there for you are so sad. But what is in this to be so sad? In fact I don't know what happened next. And dear you should remember one thing that we decided that we would never attach with anyone in any condition. You know this", Pratham trying making him memorized him about their rules about the life.

"Yes I know, we decided that we will never attach with anyone emotionally except our life partner. I also remember your words to give all our love to wife only ", Vishal made him sure that he know all rules, with so panic mood as if he wanted to tell what a stupid rule they had made. "But Pratham you know about my love for Mayuri. How much I do love her you know it. And…….." suddenly Mona, Vishal's sister, called for some religious rituals, "Vishal, come here, panditji is calling to you. And Pratham now leave your friend. After program you can seat." With big laugh she went inside.

"Ok. Vishal, you go, meet him, what new kites he is flying inside just check it!" both wanted to talk so much but unwillingly they parted from each other.

Now Pratham was seated alone on the chair looking towards all people. All are known but still he didn't want to talk with anyone. Known people also became unknown to him, how interesting it was!! He started thinking that the person living so much in others marriage ceremony how can be so much unhappy in his own marriage? Puzzle was difficult to solve without help of Vishal, so there was only way to wait for him. First time Pratham was feeling lot alone in the presence of many people without his friend. He was also unhappy inside but how could he show to the person who is the same, then who would support them.

He remember their first fight after which they both became best friends up to the college life, and surely for the whole life. Both had completed their education from the same college but in different streams. Their job made them separated from each other. Pratham got remember all the things that they did together. Among them, one thing was quiet deferent and it was Mayuri….. Pratham was piped into the past

Vishal saw Mayuri first time in the college when it was first day of their college. All village guys had not any dare to talk with any girl but Vishal was something smart than others. He could manage the situation well and could able to find out the way in any difficult situation. He was nice guy, looking handsome, fair face with simple formal living style.

Within few days he got success to make the friendship with Mayuri. But he didn't want to tell anyone except Pratham. Pratham was only person for Vishal as the safe locker for his private matters. Many times he used to say that god made him my friend to solve my pains and to guide me in hard situation.

Pratham advised him many times to propose her about his love for her, either she would say 'yes' or 'no', both were better for him, but he Vishal weren't replied anything to him about that.

Vishal was only looked her for eight years. In this way eight years passed away, still Vishal was plying the game of eyes and emotion, as he believed that he one day she would come to know about his love. But that mad fellow could not understand that nobody understand about mind. How she could? And really he was mad in her love. In reality he didn't want to give any trouble to her. He was always looking for her in the college, many times dropped his lectures and even was seating in her classes. He was roaming behind her only to see sweet smile. He was doing many things for her also without any complain. What would be the limit of love for anyone? Surely no one can believe on this simply but eight years is not a short period for anyone. We can see many boys in the college; can change eight girl friends within these eight years. In these years he never looked at anyone. In fact he had been making the plane of marriage with her after getting good job, would like to give her a surprise about this. And there was no problem cast and religion, both were liable according to their social circumstances, in the sense, they had same cast and religion.

But Pratham was not agree with Vishal's ideas about future, knew better that anything could happen in the future so it is better to do in the present. He knew about his friend but what about the girl who was unknown about the mind and emotions about the Vishal and his love. Perhaps he feared that she will engage with someone if that stupid will not say her.

So, Pratham had decided to tell her everything about Vishal and his affection for her. Pratham told Vishal everything. Pratham informed him about his notion about the topic. Vishal replied him, "Are you mad? Why is u telling her about this? I know she will come to know about my love one day."

"My dear stupid friend, how will she come to know about your love? Tell me about this. I want to know." Pratham told him.

"Sure, if my love is true, then she must come to understand, my love; I told you before that" said Vishal firmly.

"Then tell me where your love is since eight years. Is it on foreign tour or searching something? Is there answer for that?" Pratham got laugh on that.

"I think you are jealous with me Pratham. Because you don't know what is love? If you do at once then you can't ask such question to anyone. And don't dare to suspect about my love." said Vishal. There was complete silence. Nobody understood what to say but suddenly Vishal realized that his behaviour was not good for his best friend.

Vishal said, "Ok. Come with me. I will tell her everything but remember one thing my dear friend if she will discard my love I can't live without her and you will be the responsible for all the things will happened." One thing was there that whatever the condition will come; his friend would never let him die. He was indirectly committed to be stand behind him always.

Finely both friends Vishal and Pratham met to Mayuri as they decided the plan. Pratham saw her first time very closely. Rightly Vishal told Pratham was completely test less fellow about love. He was impressed with beautiful lady, her eyes, nose; lips all were so well shaped. She was well maintained healthy girl. Pratham didn't want to waste any time in the useless discursion. So, he directly came on the topic. And said her,"Miss Mayuri I want to tell you one important thing. Do you know how Vishal is?"

"Yes! I know him well. He is nice guy!" replied Mayuri to the Pratham.

"Then you should know about his love for you" Pratham gave her unexpected shock.

"What! Vishal and loves me?" "Yes. Please don't react so much. At least listen to me. You don't know that from last eight years he is in your love. And I am sure about him that he will not give chance you to complaint." Pratham was trying to convince her.

"I am sorry Mr Pratham. Your friend should know that I am not this type of girl." Mayuri replied angrily without putting any glance at Vishal, as if he had made the big crime.

"Today you said such words, it's ok but listen both of you. Don't try to flirt with me. I don't want to listen such disgusting words again neither I will call my parent. I thought he was keeping friendship with me. But what stupid he is! And listen you, don't see in surrounding also. I don't know how can you think about this thing? You are total cultureless guys. Who will love with such jokers? First make your currier and then think about love." She left the canteen and started walking out. Both had not dare to look at her even. At least they didn't want to look at her. Now Pratham could not understand how to handle the situation but he tried to make his friend relax about the situation when he saw his eyes full of tears.

Vishal was completely unable to understand what to say. Mayuri's words were blasting on his ears and making wounds on the heart. Vishal came to know why his friend was telling him to ask her about. He could not understand that was it wrong or right what his friend did for him. But one thing was cleared, Mayuri was not his love.

Years passed with the incident but the things were remain in his brain that we should do something as she told. Yes there was no any identity of him without his father's name. That day they both decided that they would never attach emotionally to anyone. But something was there which was catching them emotionally.

Meanwhile Vishal had been completed his education in MCA and joint one multinational company as the software engineer. Now his father started searching the right choice for him. Unexpectedly Vishal's father gave the invitation for Mayuri's family but when they listen that the boy have private job in Pune, they simply discarded the proposal. But this thing was unknown to Vishal and Pratham. They were happy that finally she will come in his life. Vishal got this news very late and became so much nervous. Vishal's family was ready for the marriage but her father was the breaker in the matter who expected government servant for the marriage and he was in private service.

In the matter Vishal's family could not wait they expected that the marriage should get over as early as possible. So were on the search. His father was not known about his love. Within a few days his father fixed his marriage with a well educated girl, fortunately or unfortunately he had to be ready for that. Neither he could say his father nor to Mayuri, it full of amphora. He became ready for his father's wish. To make them happy he convinced himself anyhow. He wished always that he should do something for his parent. Finally he had too sacrificed all the things including the girl whom he loves most. What he could do? Whether it was right or wrong didn't know. Simply as modern boy he could opposed for the marriage or could asked the once again. Many would both things were possible for him but he should know that he was not Romeo to tell everything. His fear about Mayuri and love for father stopped him to do so.

Vishal told all the things to Pratham what had happened before. Pratham got shocked now that what Vishal was telling and had lot worry about. Her father was ready for their marriage but why didn't his father accept that proposal? Pratham was just trying to guess the situation what might have happened before in that family but he could guess only without getting the truth. It was only Vishal who could tell him his truth. Suddenly he realised that Vishal was already seated beside him and looking at him.

Tell me one thing if her father was ready then why you didn't? Or you didn't want due to her angry words? I can't understand. But surely this can't be the reasons. What's the fact? Tell me Vishal…"he could not stop himself to ask her such words.

"Pratham, her father called to papa on the same day when I was going to engage with Bharati. We all were making preparations for the engagement ceremony. And guests were on the way. Everything was ready. Suddenly papa received the call of her father. He said that he was ready for the marriage of them and should do formalities. He invited us. But papa was in anger that how the person could tell me these things that already rejected my son's proposal. So he told everything truly to her father." Vishal told all the things, very surely in a smooth manner. Now he came to understand about the real condition of his problem.

"Then what did you decide? You should have told to your father. Uncle could understand my dear."

"Pratham I know my father. He asked me for this marriage and as you say, I got ready for it. He told all relatives that he is very happy with this marriage. This relation made families very happy, Pratham. How could I oppose? And try to understand the situation. Pratham, at least one day before also I could do something. Only one day. Pratham, one day only!" Vishal stopped his words but his eyes were speaking still with tears, looking helplessly, towards Pratham.

Suggestions, advices all things Pratham had thrown away, because all things were useless for them. He could not understand how to handle the situation. He was completely trapped in the confusion that how to tell him that he was not responsible for that all. As the same he was searching who was responsible for that problem. Both were looking towards the crowd as if they both attached their hearts to each other and trying silent conversation. They couldn't understand whether to cry or smile on the beautiful game played by his fate?

Many times they were telling to friends that nobody can make us cry. But today time and his fate made this successfully. And had made them reason, for their pain. Time played its game, now they could only find out the reasons for lifetime.

***

3

Unfortunate Love

"What do you want, sir? What can I help you sir, please? "waiter asked very pleasantly, suddenly Niles got his attention.

"Hmm! No…no… no… Nothing just waits for few minutes. I will call you back. Actually somebody is on the way when she will come I will give you order. Ok"

"Ok sir." uttered while he listened last statement and smiled very cute. He knew about the people waiting for the girls and their friends every day.

Niles became very anxious while he saw 7: 15 pm in his golden watch which was given him as gift on his 26th birthday. Actually, he got the time to meet 6:30 pm from someone. Now it's something difficult to the person who works in private sector.

Niles was teacher in well reputed English School. Still he was unmarried or waiting for his life partner. From middleclass family, two sisters, two brothers, parents, among them he was third ranker. His one elder brother got married and now searching for good house for sisters.

After school he used to take tuitions of his own school students. And today he said lie to his students that he was not feeling well so he left the class before half an hours. And now really he was not feeling well. While dozen of couple seating in on each table. Waiter was laughing from corner. Why he was laughing he knew very well. Actually, he was very angry with him but what could he do? He was seating in his restaurant.

He noticed about two beautiful couples in the restaurant. Now he started to observe them. One was pure Maharashtra who were only watching into eyes and eating snacks. Niles felt that scene like Hindi movie

How beautiful it was for him, as if they were playing with their eyes and other spectators only enjoying the movie. And other one couple was seated in the corner, newly enter college students. Girl was quite attractive and had attractive shape, wore blue jeans and purple top, adding more beauty in her natural attractive body. But on the contrary the boy was as average, not looking much handsome even. Only his appearance indicated his family background. Niles noticed that the boy had an interest only in her body, while he saw them only in objectionable condition. On the same time Niles felt jealous that he had not such a beautiful girl friend.

In this way he was started thinking to pass the time. He wanted to take something for eat but still his mind was not ready.

Suddenly waiter came to understand that he had to deliver something to in his service table no. 43 while he saw the glittering eyes of Niles. In fact waiter should be skilful in pure understand about his customer.

Niles saw his watch. It was 7:50 pm, now he wanted to ask her the correct time. First he was very much angry with her due to waiting for her from about an hour. But he satisfied himself with her arrival. Meanwhile he got many calls from many important people and family also for getting dinner. As soon as Niles asked her about the reason for her late coming, waiter interfered in their discussion

"What would you like to take madam?"

"Then who am I?"

"You o one thing, first I want one pizza... and then will take coffee. What do you want Niles?" said Taniya with rough voice. Waiter confused for minute. It was not first time for him that the girl was giving an order. But after all he had to pay the bill, he knew that.

"Bring the same pizza bhai!!!!!" Niles uttered anxiously. Now what to say he didn't understand.

"I can't think that today you will pay the bill!!"

"Who said? Are you mad?"

"You ordered it then you will pay the bill, simple."

"Isn't it felt shameful to you when I will pay the bill?" Taniya answered him with little smile.

Now Niles couldn't say anything. In fact he knew that who can win woman in the debate. Off course, No one! They have always an answer for each question.

She put her head in the mobile to see the message box. Niles, who was waiting for her from an hour, simply neglected. That's a friendship. But Niles didn't care about it because now he could see her face very closely without any difficult. Her beautiful eyes that rose petal liked lips, etc he could observe. Taniya had beautiful and attracted well maintain figure.

Taniya and Niles both met at first time in college but rooted shy natured Niles could not talk with her. He liked her much from her first look while standing in queue for filling the admission form. Then Taniya was in first year and Niles was student of third year. In college gathering time for cultural program, they came together and introduced each other. From that day Taniya started to take a help of Niles for everything, even in private life also. But she was quiet unknown or might be but Niles could not be able to express his love for her more. He hoped that one day she would understand naturally about his love.

Second thing his fear that that if she come to know that he loved her, might be angry and finish all relation. At least it is better that he could see her. He didn't care that she neglected his eyes.

Both had a good friendship. Many of among their friends taunting them personally but no one dared to tell them such things in group. Both of their families also were known about it.

"Madam, your pizza and sir it's yours" waiter inform them about their order.

Suddenly Niles got disturbed by the waiter interruption in his beautiful duty as if he was protecting her.

"Ok... Thanks" Niles said. "Welcome sir. Anything do you want madam?"

"I will call you, if we need anything. Ok" said Taniya to him

"Now will you please say me what's a problem? Now, please... leave a phone beside. You know how do I come?"

"Ya!! It's important and its serious problem" said Taniya

Niles replied "I know it's serious when you can call me only, that mean it is. Tell me now what I will do?"

She smiled and said "Niles how smart you are. You are really good."

He knew her words of flattery. He laugh to thought her trick of butter on bread before eat it.

"Actually, Niles the problem is that. My family selected a boy for me. After two days he will come but I don't want to marry before completing my currier. And you know this." She informed him.

Niles glanced at her face "then how can I help you in this? But you have to marry one day Taniya. Why don't it now?"

He said very high words but it was not simple for him. Actually he was shocked while listen the words. He really loved her from his bottom of the heart. Something it is better to say something to someone. Time never let you understand about the game of the fortune. Niles becomes so sad in deep of his heart but what to say and to do. He could not understand, in fact he controlled himself.

He came to understand about the reality that

one day she would marry someone. Today she was telling "no" for it but the answer would never be the same always.

Niles, I want your help. You know when someone would reject the girl? My family never listens to me if I said 'no'. So he should reject me."

"Ok, then tell him directly. You can meet him personally." He said confidently as if he wanted to break that.

"Yes!! But what I should say him. Proper and strong reason should be there Niles. You please find out some solutions. Why should I meet him?" hopefully she said him.

"I can meet him but can't tell him anything. No. just tells me how he would reject me. I am not going to marry him in any condition. How is the plane if I would send you in to the hospital?" When she told this beside all couples started laughing including Taniya. But there were no any type of expressions on his face.

Meanwhile Taniya had finished her pizza and wanted to order the coffee. She called the waiter by taking one piece of pizza from his plate. Waiter was watching all the things and simply could listen their discussion.

He asked her "yes madam what do you want again"

Coffee …. And what?" smiled very cute. "You can call something if you want. After all I have to pay the bill"

"Remain hungry ok. One coffee you can take."

"Ok, madam. I think you are in problem. I can understand it. If you don't mind, I have one nice solution." Waiter tried to give some idea.

"Oh!! Nice you are doing this job also? Don't you feel anything while listen such personal things of the people?" Taniya became so much angry with the fellow.

"Stop Taniya." Just wait a minute. Ok mister; say what your idea is?" Niles requested with kind heart.

Waiter started as if he was an advocate for them, "why don't you both marry? Means you can understand each other. You can be a good lover."

Niles afraid about the anger of Taniya what she would do now? He told the waiter "you please go and thank you for advice" he went with little smile.

"You please forget it. Anything he is telling, mad fellow……..Taniya, what's happened?"Taniya sank into the sea of thoughts. Niles knew that she didn't like this idea.

Niles, final! You came with me as my boyfriend. I will show you to him. We both should meet. Ok. Tomorrow we will go there. You will be ready for. ." Taniya exclaimed as it was final. She considered him without knowing what was in his mind.

Next day they decided to meet him- The boy whom she would have to married. Taniya and Niles came early but that boy – Nakul came very late. Taniya was preparing to meet him till. Taniya wanted to tell him about them.

As soon as he entered, they both saw him for first time. Taniya was fully impressed by his personality, way of speaking, his style, everything. Even she was forgotten why she called him. Simply it was beginning for her to fall in his love.

Niles tried to tell her three times but Taniya

stopped him. Niles understood that he was going to become the broker in their love rout. As their meeting stopped, they started leave each other.

She was looking quite happy. It was not very difficult for Niles to understand. Taniya said her family that she was ready for marriage, in this way her marriage was fixed with Nakul. He was in the police service so she liked him. Her family was quiet happy when they got the news that Taniya was ready for marriage. Taniya started to forget Niles slowly. But still she needed to ask him many things. Completely she could not neglect him. At least she could not. But on the other hand Niles started to neglect her because he became so sad when he listen the news of her marriage. Now he understood that he could have told her about his love.

Niles was seating silently in the company of his friends here and there Taniya was ready to enter in her new life. First time in his life he drunk wine with his friends. His friends become surprise about it that the boy who had been giving them company only, often rejected to share. But today he had taken two swipes. Suddenly he came t know that he was doing wrong while his one friend told him that he had not any love affair with Taniya. What he would get after all. He left drinking also.

He got legal invitation from Taniya. And family as well as from Nakul as he believed, Niles was the reason behind this marriage Going to be successful. On that day he remained at home only, not went to school, called his students and informed some his decisions. He discussed with his family. About his some matters, He kept his secret into his pocket what he would do in future.

Niles decided that, he would not do anything

wrong with himself but he have to do something better. After that nobody had seen him within those two days. But only he met his best friend Shalini at last day. When he was remained at home he called Shalini to meet at 'modern shopping mall'. He bought one beautiful and precious gift for Taniya with the help of Shalini. Shalini was only person who knew about Niles's love for Taniya but he took promise from her that she would never told Taniya or anyone in any condition. He discussed all the things to her. When she asked him where he was going. He answered her,"Shalini this city will not allow me to live with her memories, and I don't want to die. Hence I have to choose my way…."

How much she understood he didn't know. He handed the gift to Shalini and went away. Shalini was only looking toward him while he went. How can someone love a person who doesn't able to understand eyes of person? Shalini was thinking about it only. After all what could she say?

Taniya was looking so beautiful in bride costume; her original fair face was looking more beautiful. All were so happy Taniya as also so happy but her eyes were searching for someone into the crowd. Her all friends, relatives, affectionate met her but still she was not happy far seating Shalini was gazing her. Off course, she came to understand Tania's worry. Someone nearer and dearer, more than friend was not getting found within that known crowd. She thought to call him where he was. But unfortunately it was not possible. Pandiatji stared holly hymns. Audience was looking towards the new couple standing on the stage. And finally they blessed by the people when has completed his mantras. Now friends, colleagues, relatives started to come on the floor but, Shalini got up fast and gave one box in her hand.

She surprised about the box. Shalini was still standing. Taniya become confused when Shalini only handed the box gift box but didn't wished her about marriage. Still she said, "Thanks Shalini. What is in this big box?"

Shalini, "sorry, I don't deserve for this 'thanks' and I don't know what's in this. He gave me to pass it to you. By the way, happy marriage and hope for good married life."

Taniya got more confused to her listen her best friends rough words. She could not understand what to say now. She opened the paper on the box and read the name of sender.

"Dear Taniya, I pray to god to serve you all happy married life. Your unfortunate lover, Nilesh."

She became sad, what to do? Why she was feeling to lose everything. She felt fence down for few moments but controlled herself anyhow. Only crying was remaining. But still with dare she asked "but where is he?"

Shalini," Nobody knows about him, even his family too. Don't worry he is alive but alone."

Her last word 'alone but alone.' Were injecting her like thorns. Even after full control few tears fallen down from her ocean like because she came to know about the harsh reality whether he was unfortunate or she.

He was "alive but alone" but what about she. She became unconscious within that crowd.

***

4

Small Mistake

Life shows many new things everyday which are unable to unable to understand for any human being in simple way such things are may be possible beyond of any definition. This is the reason why we can't define the life in a particular frame. Nobody can predict his or her future what would happen in upcoming moment still we go to fortune teller for asking our future. Love is another one word which is unable to understand and difficult to define. It is the word that is good or bad for anyone to say when I saw the story of one girl who sacrificed everything for her love but what did she get from this that is the question?

This story of Nalini, a smart, attractive, well maintains figure, fare face, well educated girl, may be the complete woman. She could catch the attraction of anyone among the crowd. She was working in an IT company when her life took a tragic turn in very tragic way. Nalini was belonging to the south India. She said about her family and her village. She was the fifth child of her parent living in small town of Tamilnadu and measurable earning with little amount of money from small piece of field. Even her father was decided to make all his children well educated. So that Nalini had taken education from Chennai. When she had completed primary education,she took education at Chennai. She was quiet intelligent girl and having good sense so many people requested to her father to let her education complete from distant place from their less progressed village area. So she completed her education in Chennai. After that she came to Pune, Maharashtra to search out some opportunities to build her currier.

It is well known that Pune is the mother land of all knowledge. It is historical city and had seen many vital incidents of history and faced many attacks of various rulers. It messages us to fight with the condition. Many important figures in freedom movement were belonged to Pune. Even great Maratha Empire took its first breath in Pune region. Such affectionate city could not discard Nalini. It's the reality that hundreds of people come every day to check out job opportunities. Nalini came there to know how she could get job with the help of her university friends. Finally she got the job due t her skills and good knowledge.

Finally she settled somehow, with the good salary she started living her good life. She had one sister and two brothers behind her, were taking education in village. Slowly Nalini took all their responsibility upon her shoulder. She started sending all type of help to her family without fail. Her father told her when she left for Pune that she should take care of herself due to his extreme fear about unknown city and keep all limitations but loneliness kills man, man can't live with complete satisfaction. She sometimes disturbs to see her friends with their boyfriends in miserable condition. Up to that she kept safe distance with male friends because she knew about her family. She always had feared that if she do anything wrong what answer she would give to her family, especially to her lovely father. She could not think about love or such mad things or didn't want to any cultural impact on her.

One day she was going to company when waiting for the bus on bus stop. She noticed to a boy was gazing her with hungry eyes. She neglected towards him. She understood by his fashionable but awkward appearance that he was one of the vagabond guys among his friend. But she couldn't understand why her mind was attracted towards the fellow. Suddenly the bus came and she left for but still the boy was watching her with evil smile. It was the first day when any face reflected in her mind. Whole day she was thinking about him and his smile. In fact she was perplexed about whether she had anger or affection.

After passing a night while made herself ready for the office, her eyes were searching that boy around the bus stop but this she replied the boy with smile against of her artificial anger, she tried to neglect the boy but it was too late, he was successful in his game and green signal he got for the next level. Today she gathered the courage to neglect him somehow. Little bit she doubted about him and wanted to quarrel with him but she controlled herself by convincing why she would dispute, only he was watching her which was common thing in metro city life. She left the place with her daily bus. Now Nalini was watching him only so his daring was started up and finally one day he came and seated beside Nalini in the bus. It was clear they started to follow her. First Nalini was in fear to see the boy who was following her from last station, she gazed him slowly, she shocked, and he was watching her with very lustful eyes as if he would eat her within few minutes. She started looking out of the window. But her complete attention was only towards the sensitive activity of body, which was playing the game of sensibility. Within some time the stop came and she tried to leave the bus, in that hurried moment the boy touched her private part. She suddenly felt shameful, a first male touch to her body made her uncomfortable. Rationally she left that event, as she wanted to beat him, slap him, but she could not. When she came out of the bus, the boy was watching towards her and saying sorry by holding his ears. All anger turned into laugh and laughing burst out.

Form that day they started t meeting each other, connected on phone and so on, they started coming close. In simple way their love story started. She came to know about him. His name was Rakesh, graduated in arts faculty from university of Pune. His father was an engineer in well known company. Totally his family background was good as he told to the Nalini. Nalini believed him without knowing any reality. It was 31stdecember when she served herself to him. First time came to know about woman within her. She felt all the emotions of woman. Now she madly fell in love with him. Unintentionally her concentration towards him parted her to neglect her job even. There Rakesh wanted this only and he confirmed that he had caged her in his love nest. He knew one thing that Nalini was working in Well Company on good wages, so she was cash account for him. Nalini started to do all expenses for him he had no any job, fully vagabond. Nalini told him may times that he should do something for his own spend. From their first physical encounter they started living together because he became her physical need and she depended on him for her physical appetite. Therefore Nalini had surrendered herself emotionally and physically in the hands of Rakesh. Nalini had some savings for her emergency. She bought one flat for them. Now Nalini started to see dream of her marriage with Rakesh still had no any job and totally he was depended on her for any expenses. Again she hadn't dared to ask him about his family.

That day she decided to surprise him to give the news of the flat where nobody could ask them any question and freely they can enjoy their love. She entered in the room and got shocked to see something unexpected in her room. Two wine bottles on table, empty snack packets, and other things. Where was Rakesh? She found him in drunken state. She could not tolerate smell even. She shocked when the call came, "Nalini beta, what happened? You told me that you will give me thousand rupees. You would have to send me today at noon. I was at home only due to your words, but nobody came. Her room owner was there who wanted to know about the rent of his house. Now Nalini came to understand what might have happened.

"Sorry uncle I forgot, but I will pay it. I am extremely sorry, uncle."

"Ok beta! I do believe on you. See Nalini if any problem is there, you can tell me without fail. How are you? And see don't forget that your one uncle is there. My child, Take care."

'Yes uncle. Thanks!! I will take care. Bye"

After two days when Nalini was working on laptop but still she was not completely concentrated on her devoted work because company had given her a responsibility of very important project. But ringing doorbell brought in the conscious world. Then she disclose the entrance door little ajar to see who was standing out what make her surprise, Rakesh was standing outside of the door.

The curtain fell down to disclose his character and nature but she didn't feel fair to wake up him but she decided to talk on the issue at the morning but how could she sleep. Her disturbed mind was thinking about Rakesh only. Somehow she passed the night. Early in the morning when she woke up, she found that Rakesh already left the house. She didn't know when she got sleep at night with t

Thinking about Rakesh, She prepared herself for office. She could not believe on her eyes while passing to see Rakesh with his friends smoking a smoking a cigar on local shop she didn't want to talk with him but still she was looking towards him. Rakesh informed by his one friend that his girl friend was looking him so quickly he threw away his cigar on the road and turned back to meet Nalini but within a moment bus came and Nalini took the bus and left.

After two days, when Nalini was working on the laptop but still her whole concentration was on the devoted work given by the company , all responsibilities were led upon the shoulder of very important project of the company. Suddenly door bell rang which brought her into conscious world. She opened the door, what a surprised that Rakesh was standing outside. For a moment she felt to shut the door immediately but before she could the act; Rakesh spoke out his pardoned words. "Nalini I'm really sorry. Please forgive me. Sorry my dear. Wont you allow me enter in the house?"

She took him inside and closed the door meanwhile Rakesh tried to hold her arms but she refused at first of his trial by annoying him,"please don't touch me. Live me alone."

"I am sorry Nalini. Actually on that day I was feeling very sad. You don't know how much I was in tension about the job. In that tension I had………….." he started weeping sorrowfully. "I didn't want hurt you my dear. I am guilty for that but you can give me the punishment for that, But except depart from you my dear. I can't live without you."

"But why did you spend that amount what I gave you to pay the rent of the room." Nalini asked him.

He exclaimed, "Yes! But that bloody fellow told me that I am living on your money. In that anger I made the mistake and liquored. He badly told me about our relation." He started weeping like a trained actor.

Confused Nalini could not understand what to do? She melted like soft candle in front of warmness of his love. She hugged him to her breast with words. "Ok I can understand your condition. Actually I forgot to tell you the news that from next month we are going to shift from this flat to our own flat but……"

"What? You have bought flat for us….. Means you! And see Nalini! How I am bad that couldn't give you a small gift even." He said measurably.

"Hey! Are you mad? Is there anything that departs us? And belong to me anything that is yours because you are mine only. And if you are talking about the job, Mr. Rakesh you will get it one day sure." She told in advancing manner.

"You have given me good news! Let's celebrate come my dear!!" lift her in arms and both went into the bedroom to celebrate the moment. At the midnight tie when both had tired, Nalini noticed the right time to discus about the marriage

"Rakesh I think we should get marry now. How much time we will live likes this?" Nalini said.

"Who do you afraid to? Is there any problem?" he uttered.

"No, I think we should get marry as early as possible." She said him. But maybe he didn't want to understand.

"What are you talking about my dear? Are you ok? Actually I don't want such restrictions of marriage bonds."

"I will not put any restriction to you. But when my friend and relatives will ask me about the relation between you and me, what I would say to them? That who are you my boyfriend or playboy?" she said strict forwardly.

"Oh!!Nalini sorry!! I understand your problem. I will do anything for you, just tell me what to do?" he changed his way of talking when Nalini told him strictly.

"Means you are ready for marriage? Thanks but first I want to meet you parents then we will do next." She put new problem in front of him.

"Nalini I think we have to do everything without

them. We should make habit of their absence." He became quiet abnormal but Nalini handled the situation. And she said, "Ok. Don't worry! We will meet them another time. I am sure they will accept as their daughter in all."

"I hope but tell me, will your family accept me?" now her face became so pale with many worries. Thought of her family made her quiet embarrassed but suddenly she tried to compromise him.

"When I will say them you will get a god job and you are my choice how can they reject you my dear? But promise me one thing that you will leave drinking and I don't like your friends too."

"Ok my Janu! As you wish. But we need them up to our marriage." both started laugh and lost into their dream of marriage. Especially Nalini was so happy due to the lovely behaviour of Rakesh but on the same time had some worries too in her mind.

Within few days Nalini and Rakesh both had completed all the rituals and the legal process of registration of court marriage. And as they expected their marriage was got over. In that pleasure both arranged the small feast to call their friends and colleagues. All enjoyed the party and gave best wishes to them on the occasion of party and for better future life. But one unexpected thing had happened which was completely unexpected to the Nalini. Her one friend Sarita left her party in full of anger when she met to the Rakesh. Rakesh didn't say anything on the matter what had happened.

But she asked him with full of courage, "Rakesh do you know Sarita?"

"Who is she? I don't know any girl with this name. But why are asking this question?"

"Dear don't you remember the girl left our party just now? I thought she met to you before leave."

"Oh! That girl name is Sarita. And you mean did she go because of me?"

"Why do you so embarrassed. I am just asking you about her. Not blaming you to be the responsible for her departure away from party."

"Just leave Nalini. Today is our honeymoon and I don't want it to waste. Let's celebrate my dear life. Some another day we will discuss this matter and as her about." he memorized her about the event.

Near about one month Nalini and her husband Rakesh lived very happy married life. One most important thing was happened for the Nalini that Rakesh told her that he got the job and even started for going. But ones she shocked to see Rakesh in drunken condition with his friends. He told her about the force of friends for the wine. Such many things he said her. But Nalini scared about his daily routine. Now Rakesh started to take drink and most ridiculous thing was his promise at each morning not to drink. She embarrassed about the condition. Now it was time when the condition started drove out from her control. Everything started going out of her hand.

Many things were started sliding out of her hands because many he was telling lie, still her love for him could not reduced. It was Sunday when she said him for going to see movie but he discarded her saying about official work and left the house. Evening she decided to go out for trip, she saw that Rakesh was roaming with girl, quit more beautiful than her. Now she couldn't understand what to do. Any woman can't bear the lady with her husband that same she was feeling to kill her husband but on the other side her brain remained silent in front of her heart. She decides to follow them and up to 8'PM she followed them and stopped their track when they entered into the lodge. How could she mislead? She returned to the home but with tearful eyes which was the clear sign of repentance of her life. She knew that she could not do anything with the Rakesh. For a moment she falls in the thought of suicide but she left the thought again. Suddenly she remembered about the Sarika, her one friend.

After two days, Nalini asked him when both were taking breakfast early in the morning, "Rakesh, you really don't know about Sarika?" her question was direct attack on Rakesh.

"Nalini, dear again you started joke. "He replied.

"I am not joking. I am serious about your profession. I visited to your company. But they told me that no any person, name Rakesh, is working in their company."

"What do you mean everything I should do with your permission?" he shouted as if he was criminal.

"I don't care now. Just tell me, how many girls life do you ruin Mr. Rakesh? And tell me what my number is?"She becomes so much panic with his answer.

"You.. Stupid bitch!! You are the same like other mad women. I really love you and you are talking about my character. Tell me what you have done for me? I left everything what I had only because of you, in your love. If you don't believe me then please tell me, I will not come in your life again. I am going bye." He was showing himself as she was ingratitude for his did for her.

"What are telling mad fellow? You gave me

everything. Shameless person I gave you everything. I left everything for you and now you are telling me this. I know about you doll, who is giving you all sexual pleasure. Listen, now it will be better for you, if you will not come to me again. I don't want to see your face. Don't show me your face again, you cheater, liar. Get lost from my house." she started crying. Now he came to know that no use of his discussion.

She felt that her stomach was paining and unbearable. It was unbearable to her. She called her neighbour. First time she was feeling womb pain. She got great shocked when doctor informed her about pregnancy, it was most horrible moment for her. She was confused whether to live or to die. She started crying while remembered about Sarika, thought to become second Sarika.

One month after she got another shocked when told her friend to take out some money, but her account had no money. Actually many had advised her for the abortion but only mother can understand about the emotional attachment with her child. Other can only give the suggestion. She wanted to give birth to that child.

Sarika came to see her in her wardroom and saw her condition. Really the child was very nice. But all three were disgusted to see each other but Nalini came to understand that it was part of her flesh. Vidya informed her that Rakesh was eloped with a college girl to the Kashmir and withdrew all her 3 lakh rupees from her account. But Sarika was helping her for all the things. Vidya was telling all the things about him but Sarika and Nalini both were just listening about it and looking at the child only. As if both had the same pain, why not? The source was the same for the pain.

Sarika started telling her, "Don't remorse yourself please, Nalini. You did pure love as I did. That selfish person didn't understand this pure love. Such people should punish. Fight for this, I am always with you. Take care. Bye.

Nalini went into depressed mind. What after that? What she could do? But she knew how to live. One small mistake divested her life. No doubt she was the best model for those who do the same things what she did. It was difficult for her to ride on the problem. She knew that whatever game her fate played with her, whatever result was. But ……show must go on!!

***

5

Othello Revised

It is really amazing about our universe that the scientist have found many unbelievable things in the universe, that's unbelievable to us. On the same time everyone lives in his own created unnatural and imaginative world which is always unknown to the mortal world. This imaginary world is always unseen to anyone except nature which many times strike on this world. Generally we are unable to understand about nature. As if we all are puppets in the hand o the fortune and it plays with us till it's getting bore, it laughs when we weep while it gives us slap. Many times innocent have to also suffer without their any fault from its treatment.

But on the same it also performs the roll of the guide to show them the right way to the humanity. Nature is the judge who gives a better result for any type of fault has done by the human being without wasting the time. Many people understand it but after getting punishment.

What crime was done by the Nayana? Today also Sandip trying to understand about the incident what had happened with him. Today even after two years Sandip doesn't ready to repent on his crime. He is into the jail as if he had done nothing wrong to killed anyone whom we love than any other person, due to single tragic flaw. He was trying to tell all that it was her mistake, not his. But God knows what the reality was. Many time men don't understand the woman, about her mind, love for us, and greatness of her mind. She is the only thing after the God who creates the world again. If we can understand him at least fifty percent, we will be equal to the God.

The story is about the Sandip and anyone, who was married before three years and came together. Sandip was software engineer and started his work in Mumbai. He was good and matured guy who was very much happy with his life. He was belonged middle class farmer's family who were doing work on the small piece of land got from the ancestry. His father believed that his children should be more educated to stand their own legs that would make them suffered as they were suffered in the farming. It is the naked fact about the farming sector that how difficult it is become. Sandip was good student in his school time but he would like to live alone and didn't want to talk with anyone in the school. He was totally attic one and like this he became. Only he had made friends in the college and on his workplace. Hence, there was no one where he could have opened his mind and his feelings. It's a natural truth that friend is only place where we can open our mind and feelings, he is always important in the life. They can make you free and true friend can read your eyes what you have in your minds. They always remove your faults of the life and the personality. Even up to the college life he hadn't any smell of love or any affection about the girl. But he had an attraction for one girl in the college but due to his introverted nature he was unable to express his love to the girl.

We have always some turning points in the life, same he also introduced with girl who changed his life and came like the natural gift. But In reality we know, everyone does not get such lovely gift in the life and person who gets it, surely a lucky one. Nayana was the name of the colour who decorated his life from each of the corner of the life. She was the beautiful girl for Sandip. She was a gorgeous looking, smart, intelligent girl from Gujarat working in Mumbai. She was belonged to the rich and well educated and rich family, a daughter of typical Gujarati businessman, fell in love with Sandip.

She had taken an education from Gujarat in computer engineering. Fortunately she got the job in the software company. She was like to the Sandip only because of his nature and behaviour with the colleagues and the co-workers in the office. She was impressed by his personality. His mute, intelligent and smart of nature t lead with responsibilities of the company. Finally she fell down in love. On the other side he also liked her this fair lady and wanted to express his love but also had fear if she would be objected then what to do which was already noticed by the other staff about their behaviour while they started to talk each other.

One of his friend made his joke one day when anyone was absent at office, he had completely nervous and unhappy mood due to he made lot mistake in his work of official file. How his boss had annoyed him and how he had made many mistakes and so on. But In fact each one understood about the reason of his madness; the absence of Nayana. But when next day Nayana came and said him "Kem cchho Sandi? I was missing you lot yesterday." all saw the secret smile on his face and corrected all his work mistaken yesterday. How fantastic it was when for Sandip when they both had a secret meeting after office and even Sunday was reserved for each other. Nayana had the respect about his family and praise about their hard work in the farming. She was ready to make him the life partner but she could not understand how she could propose him while he was not showing any type expression due to his introverted nature. They both haven't proposed each other till their boss haven't called them into the office. Now how can anyone accept any relation based on the doubts? They were telling anyone that they had only friendship while asked them about their closed talking eyes.

Their untold love story reached one day inside the cabin and boss called them inside. They both haven't any idea, thought that boss called for some casual reason. Sandip and Nayana were standing in front of boss looking very eagerly.

Boss said "I want your resign letter; anyone can give me resin letter." It was shock for both of them. How he could tell such nonsense thing. Nayana replied, "but what is happened, sir? Are you joking? We are good workers and working good. We have good performance." Said Nayana but Sandip was in dilemma.

"Miss Nayana, I don't like my workers are roaming anywhere in the city. It is the question of prestige of our company that you are spoiling in the markets."

"But sir, it's our personal matter and we are good friends. All does know it." Sandip said.

"Good friends? Ha….. haa… haa. Are you joking Sandip? oh. Good joke, I like it."

"Are you only good friends? Nayana tell me the truth."

Yes sir, of course"

Boss, "Nayana will marry me. I really love you from the first day you came for the interview. "

"Mind your language Mr. Kumar? Isn't your brain on the place? She is mine and I love her……… "said Sandip and suddenly stopped himself. It was spontaneous reaction by him; even he also didn't know what he was told. Nayana was shocked by these words. She was looking surprisingly towards him what to say? On the other side Sandip was speechless with that criminal act supposing himself as convict by telling such words against of Nayana who were calling him best friend. What she would think? There was only person who was laughing, their boss who had started microphone for the other worker

Sandip understood when it when outside the cabin all was laughing.

Boss, "see Miss Nayana and you were telling me that he is only your friend and doesn't love you. Means it was trap by them all Sandip felt shy with thinking.

"Mr. Sandip I am sorry but you don't know, she also loves you lot. And I am already engage yar! She will kill me"

All started laughing. Both were silent, unable to

talk any word. "ok! Now take the decision fast of the marriage. Call to your families and discus with them. And you r tell her about your love. Propose her yar! Neither I will do it, understand." He started laughing

Sandip, "Nayana I love you. Will you marry me?" Nayana smiled and hugged very tightly.

Within few days they got married and started living together In a flat gifted by company. They were really happiest couple that moment when they first time knew, felt pure sensation of each other. they spent satisfied night with each other by mixing each other which everyone expects in the life. Great love needs great care. Nayana was open minded girl so she had contact with all type of people as the profession worker. However some days were passed very nicely for both of them.

When you do the job, you must avoid your work to bring at home, if you do so will not able to give time to your partner. Same mistake Nayana did. She was clever and well understanding girl. She thought that they were working in the place so she could get solutions on her problems and possible to improve their skills of work. But that poor girl did not know what her husband wanted?

Here Sandip wanted to feel her more and love her more but she was always been engaged herself in office works. He thought that she was neglecting him. Now it was natural for him that he was thinking this, his over passion and born fear made him started thinking about her negative side. He had doubt about her character. He had fear that she was going away from him. He also thought that he was able to satisfy her or not. Such many nonsense questions were knocking at the door of his heart and at last he opened the door and gave space them in his heart. His nature was very attic and alone. He started to be silent for each time. Nayana had already in tension or work made him.

This fear and care anyone could see clearly when she was talking someone. When you have any questions, it Is better to discuss with your partner but Sandip was not this type of man. He could not understand what to do. And no one was there who could convert him from such mad things.

Once Nayana was asking some queries but refused to tell her about anything. She knew that he was in the problem but she didn't ask him about his problem, might be she would not get answer. She noticed his aggravated nature of behaviour, maybe it was due to work load. She didn't want to disturb him. she was talking with her friend for more work. Actually she started more work, had to talk with her friend in open park. She told him about her work for their self house but he thought she was trying to show him inferior.

She was coming with her friends; so many times she was getting late at home that was also the problem for him. He had no any break from office to home but she was talking with friends after office so she was coming late. Now it's natural thing for them that they talk up to late night, without this they can't sleep. Once, many women were seating in group. They were discussing many things, as if it is their chatting club. Then, how could Nayana be the exception for this? That stupid thing led him towards another way to another way.

His fear turned into the jealousy when she was talking about her male friends. In fact he had to accept that they were living in corporate world where he had to live with liberated mind. He didn't like when she was talking with anyone. He was thinking that his wife was deceiving him and had feared that she someone would take out her from him. he said nothing to her but looking her each activity with doubtful eyes. There is no need of any ghost when already you have created ghost around you.

He was hardly irritated when anyone was talking about his wife in the office; could not bear the flattery about his wife, suddenly becomes so much anxious about the things.

Nayana got the award as the best employ of the company but he had the idea that his wife got the award in illegitimate way; he had not congratulated her for this important moment. Every husband should know that there is always her support in their success. It was not meaning that he hated her but that was only because of his over love for her. He didn't want to miss any chance to love her but sometime made many mistakes. But it was his fear and doubts stopped him to do so. His fortune started to play game with him. it is sure, when the rain of love stops, home becomes dry and barren.

In the same time on person came in their life like matchstick fallen down into the dry forest. Sharad, a software engineer from UP, started working in the same company to who company had provided the flat in the same apartment, where Nayana and Sandip were living. Sharad was good guy and just before few got married. But didn't bring his wife there because of his parents wish to keep their daughter in law with them for some days. So he started his living alone and again he had to live for six months for his wife up to his well settlement. He was good guy to talk with anyone therefore shortly he became famous for everyone in the whole building.

But Sandip was only person who were not talking more with him, in fact he Sandip was like this who didn't like to talk with anyone. But unfortunately it was Nayana who started talking with him only because of their same working place. He was younger than her. In few days Sharad and Nayana became good friends. Nayana had sympathy for him that how he was living without his wife and also appreciated about his skills in work. Once Nayana said Sandip about this that how this person can live without his wife? But Sandip was became so angry about, said "I don't know how this fellow lives without his wife, but my wife should not go there." Nayana shocked and became nervous with this arrogant answer. But she took it as a fun only and left the matter. But each day she was facing the same irritating wines of his doubts very softly.

Now Sharad also was started taking interest in Nayana but Nayana was well known about the limits. This thing Sandip noticed very easily but how could he tell her this thing. he started more and more about their relation what they have. He made the complete thought that Nayana and Sharad both were had an affair. Many times he started calling her 'where is she and with whom?'

It was first time when they both fought very aggressively and the reason was only Sharad when she called Sharad to repair their TV and happily he repaired it. Now it is the hospitability to ask any guest about the tea. Happily Nayana told him to take the tea till Sharad was watching TV. So it was the readymade reason for him and burst out his volcano of anger on Nayana. From that day he was keeping watch on their activities; especially on the Nayana. In fact he would have to think positively. Nobody can change your mind while it has negative thoughts. Now from that day Nayana started to control her point of view and her open nature.

She was not so stupid to understand his behaviour. But their life took new turn without any quarrel. He has started silent war in the house. It's natural that when the communication between two people having problem, third person takes it advantages. Same Sharad had started taking advantages from their problem. He misunderstood about Nayana frank behaviour.

It was black day of their life when Sandip had ordered to attend the business meeting of the company at Delhi as the representative behalf of the company. He had to go before two for the registration for the program. Manisha, shashank and his boss Mr. Roshan were in the team. He left the house but how could the doubt of his mind leave the house. It was evening when he left the house for the flight.

There fortune played little game in the form of Sharad wanted to eat meet but he was unable to prepare the recipe. So he decided to request Nayana to make it prepare.

He rang the bell of the door. "Good evening Mrs... Nayana."

"Oh! Sandip. Good evening, what is happened?"

"Nothing is special. Actually, I need your help. I brought meet but unable to make it."

She could understand what to say him. But she thought why shouldn't help this poor guy when Sandip was went outside. "Ok bring it. I will cook it."

"Thank you, madam" he gave her the all material. She started cooking while he was seated in the hall watching TV. Unfortunately Sharad wanted to go for washroom. He asked her about washroom. She didn't know what was in his mind. When he entered in the washroom at the same time somebody rang the bell. Nayana could not guess about it. She got shock when she opened the door; it was Sandip standing outside of the door. Nayana was became statue to think about how to handle that situation when Sandip seated in the sofa. Suddenly, Sharad came out from the washroom. Sandip became so hyper, could not control on him.

"What are you doing here? You bloody fool. Means my doubt was right. You both are enjoying in my absence."

"Mind you tongue. Sandip? What are you telling?"

"What? You should be guilty about your infidelity. Can't I satisfy you bitch? Therefore you are engaged in such dirty relation. "

"Sandip control you." Sandip said.

"Sandip you must go. It's our personal matter" Nayana trying to convince him.

"Wow. What a safe game you are playing. And what is personal now. Why are sending him outside. He will use my wife and I will leave him? No!!!"

Sandip started beating to Sharad, Sharad went out. But Nayana came in his hand. Started beating to the Nayana very angrily as if he was taking revenge of her disloyalty. Nayana suddenly went in the kitchen where Sandip got knife and unknowing stabbed in her stomach and in full of anger he stabbed tree time. Nayana fallen down on the floor like lifeless doll.

Sandip sat in the hall. He didn't know what he had done. He came to know but it was too late. Sharad called the police. Sandip became quite could not understand how he killed the lady. That time only one thing was remaining; it was remorse on his crime. Still today he is repenting on his made mistake and telling his story.

***

6

Love Is Friend, Philosopher And Guide!

"Money is not god but it is not less than god" it's true for some people who control their behaviour under their rules of the money. Parents are always ready to do anything for their children but when the issue of their marriage comes their ego always on the top about caste, realign, status, education, economical background and so on such many things comes in their mind. Sometimes they understand but that time it gets late and throw their children in misfortune.

Vikram Desai came to know about the same satire of the time and injured with the big slap of the fortune. Well-known builder in the Mumbai, His name was sufficient for any type of problem in the city, even at police station, hospital, and moll, anywhere he had an impression. The owner of 12 hundred cr. Property, don't believe on God, not even have been seen in any temple since last 20 years. But today it was surprising topic for everyone.

Mr. Desai was standing in front of the God Dhanvantary with joined hands, prayer on lips and tears in poor eyes. What did force him to bring the hospital? All were looking at him how he was waiting each second for the decision and the news form the doctors. His only son was in the operation theatre and still it was going. Satyam was his only son, whom he loved so much. After all he was the only caretaker and heir of his empire.

This is the story of Satyam, started before two years. Satyam was the child of very rich parent for whom the money was like water, no any important they give to anything then money. Satyam was grown up in very aristocratic conditions. Hi parents were always busy in parties and such modern social activities, that's why nobody was there who could take care of his nurturing, to improve his behaviour, nature. So in the course of time he also became like them and engaged in modern activities like parties, pub, night club, drinking, playing cards became his interesting activities. There for any one could found him in drunken state at any time, even at day time also. Because no one was there to tell him what was good or bad. Mother was always engaging in the shopping and parties and his father was in busyness and tours.

It was very cold day of the winter and any one

could feel so much cold on that day. On that day Satyam wanted to go outside with his friends. He was become late because he woke up very late due to last late night party. His all friends were waiting for him in the college, all were known about his activity and habits but what could they do? He was the bank for them and who would not wait for the bank. It was the time of morning, near about 10 am. When he drank little wine, he took his bike and left his house. He was good and well trained bike rider but all are familiar with the crowd and the conditions of the Indian roads especially in Mumbai. He was riding his bike on full speed as if his father had gifted that road to him on his birthday. And the unfortunate thing had happen which was not expected. He crashed his bike on a passerby, a young girl; he could not control his bike. He parked his bike beside when people gathered there around him. He was unable to understand what to do.

Satyam haven't seen such hazards of the public crowd around him when they get angry. He was complete unfamiliar with the experience how public pours its anger on someone. And after all it was a matter of girl. Satyam was became unconscious about the condition that was in front of him but when you are in problem always happened good things with the bad incident. Some good people advised him that he should take the girl in to the hospital for good treatment because she went in unconscious condition but still alive and that was better for the Satyam. He took the girl without watching her face. He didn't care about this because he came to understand her middle class family status through her appearance. Doctors admitted the girl but not ready to do the treatment on the girl because they believed that something was wrong happened with the girl, there for the girl was complete unconscious. So they told Satyam, "its police case we can't do anything without the FIR" but suddenly when he told about his father and who was he, doctors changed their mind and started the treatment but after all they call the police.

They didn't want to trap in the matter. Before that they called Mr. Vikram Desai and informed him about the accident that was done by his son. Satyam had no care for anyone before that but at the first time he became more apprehensive and worrying today; because it was the issue of his father's prestige and mostly of his own currier. First time in the life he was repenting on his any mistake when one of his friends told him about the seriousness of the matter. He stayed at hospital more than four hours. Fortunately that girl came into the conscious, her parents and police both came there. Her parents wanted to scold on him for his mistake but someone already told them about Satyam and his family condition. So these poor fellow got silent on the matter and could not tell anything to the Satyam on hi mistake only because of the fear if he do something wrong with them and had an expectation for better treatment for their child. But here Satyam was under pressure what the girl would tell to the police, he was even unaware about his condition; still his mouth smelled of strong brand of the wine. And that reason was sufficient for putting him into the jail.

Police went into her room to get information for the FIR. They strictly prohibited to the Satyam entering in the ward. But he had fear about all the things. First time he saw her face through the glass window. She was not so beautiful but her glittering innocent eyes, her normal but fresh face, and more than that her simple living style, looking nice for her condition. He was completely fascinated. He was surprise to see her so much calm and quiet, how can someone remain as calm after such dangerous accident? She told that it was her mistake to fallen on the bike. She had not given any claim on the boy. She said that the boy was n he right path only she could not listen the horn of the bike. Unwillingly police went away with the statement, without having any charge.

He came to know how the girl was, her polite and humble mind. Surely she could blackmail him or caught him into the charge and ready to get lot money for his mistake but she didn't do anything. Those things were increase respect for the girl in his mind. First time in his life, he wanted to say sorry to someone. He had been seen many people fighting for money and property, cheating even to brother and full o ego, but what he saw today was really amazing.

Now really he wanted to meet the girl and pardoned for guilt but many questions were in his mind such like what to speak with her? Will she listen? Whether she will talk or not? He had taken the permission to meet her. Till the moment his wine was came down and the effect was finished.

It was the time from last 5 hours, in which he was normal and in the condition talking someone properly. Finally he entered in the room with lot fear and said, "Hi…..I am Satyam…. Satyam Desai."

"Nice to meet you."

"How are you felling now?"

"Yes! Now it is better."

"I am really sorry what I did. I really feel guilty for fault"

"It's ok Mr. Satyam. I know you were in alcoholic

pleasure but Mr. your pleasure could have killed me, yet it gave me lot pain. You had broken all the rules of the road. This is public property and all are going from there. I hope next time will be careful while riding the bike. And all are equal on the planet everyone loves itself as you are."

Satyam realized that he had done big crime and surely it wasn't forgivable to anyone, he stood there like hanging bag. There was complete silence for few minutes, nobody could talk.

"Don't you feel that I should get punished? ……….. By the way why did you lie to the police? Why did you save me?" Satyam told to the girl looking in her eyes as if expecting an answer. He didn't think she would tell him something that would change his life forever.

"See Mr. Satyam, whether I feel to punish you but really will it come in action? No. I know you made the mistake but it is just mistake not a crime. You are only and lovely child of your rich parents. He will save you on any cost then what is the use of my complaint. Actually it is not your mistake, nobody taught you how to behave and about the culture and social etiquettes. Sorry Satyam but parent should nurture their child properly, it's their duty to teach everything to the child but unfortunately your parent forgot this as if they thought everything they can get by money. In this age you should think about your currier and take hard work for making your own identity while you are satisfied to enjoy on your father's property. Tell me Satyam what is the use of such life when you are depended on your father's name. I know what I am telling it's not bearable to you but I am just showing you the mirror." Silently she made dangerous statement but surprising thing was that Satyam was listening silently without any disturbance. Nobody had dared to talk him such things about his parents but today he met a person who told him without any fear. Each word was stroking on his heart as they were trying to open the door of his heart that was closed since years and didn't open for anybody's suggestion. They were making wounds on his mind for few minutes. Once again they were in the silence. Again her words made eco sound in the room when she realized that she said something in high pitch.

"Sorry Satyam, I think I told you something wrong. I think you should understand the life. It's a reality of rich family child. They don't care for anyone; don't know how to behave with others. They don't have any value of others' life in their eyes. Such child can't make their own identity and always troubling to others. I hope you will understand what I am telling."

Girl told very hard words in cool and soft language. Every word was entering and drilling on his brain while his eyes were fixed on her face as if he was statuette by she made magic. Nobody had been told him such things when first time he realized about what type of life he was living. Respect increased in his mind while he had to be angry with the girl for the hunting words. Satyam could not understand what to say.

He went out without giving any reaction perhaps he was deeply insulted. He paid all bill on the counter and strictly instructed to take care of her and not to give any trouble her about money or anything. He went out from the hospital and started walking on the pavement where had been seen baggers and poor people walking. First time he was walking on the road, Rich to the public bus stop and caught the bus. He knew about this while his friends were travelling by bus. He switched off his mobile. Nobody could believe that he was travelling by bus but he didn't know where to go? What to do? No any answer. Finally at the evening he reached to the Juhoo beach where he came hundreds of times but this was quite different, quietly seated on the soft sand looking towards every wave as if each wave was trying to say him something. Today the ocean was looking like that girl to him and the same words she was telling. That great ocean also would shy in front of her great heart. Now it was time to surrender in front of his bad habit. He went in the wine shop and called to the waiter and gave the order of one his regular brand. Within a few minutes he served him wine bottle. Satyam poured wine in glass, as soon as he starts to drink; his hands were started shivering as if the glass were fallen down. He could watch his father's money in the glass; respect, identity, existence of the life. Such words were storming in his mind. He sat there more than an hour only looking towards the glass and the bottle, in front of the table. After half an hour waiter informed him that was time to closing the shop. He left the shop without drinking the wine but paid the bill for.

Satyam didn't meet anyone for three days after that incident. Girl got the discharge from the hospital. All friends and parents were more surprised, what was happened with him? Where was he? Why was he so sad? He didn't make any contact with anyone even his parents were like unknown for him while at home. Now only that girl was important for him he wanted to meet her and say thanks for her good words. But he dint know her name: so went to the hospital and got her name. She was now very important for her because she was only girl who told her everything real and fact, shown him the mirror of reality. That day, he waited for more than two hours out of her office to meet her. Finally he saw her coming out from the office where she was working. He ran towards her but she didn't notice him or wanted to notice but how could Satyam stop him.

"Hi!! Supriya ……." She surprised when her name listened. More than he encountered on the way.

"Hi!! ……..." replied him as a formality but without any sweetness in the words." What happened now? Is there any problem?"

"I went to hospital but they informed that you got discharge so I wanted to know how you are..."

"Oh I am sorry actually I should inform you. Thanks for the payment. By the way I am fine."

"Now you are taunting me. In fact I should say you thanks to save me. I am really guilty for my mistake."

"It's ok. I forgot that incident; yet it was so dangerous for me. feeling happy to see you like this." He interrupted his speech.

"It's only because you Supriya I really got my mistake. If you don't mind can we go for the coffee, please? If you were forgave me."

"Ok. But only for ten minutes, actually my parents wait for me at home."

"Ok and thanks." They both were gone in the coffee house besides the side where he ordered two coffees.

"Supriya actually I am really thanks for what you told me in the hospital. You told right and I know that I haven't any manner to talking with anyone; in fact nobody taught me this. My parent didn't teach me anything learnt one thing from them that nothing is there which can't be selling but you should know its price. And among my friends also no one who could told me such things, may be they feared about me. My parents didn't have time to teach about the behaviour and manner. But you have shown me the reality. Will you be my friend….please…? I want your help. I came to know that I was wrong but I want to improve now but don't know how." Satyam tried to make her convince. Supriya said nothing. She took coffee and finished. She came to understood something that was not good. She got afraid for a moment because Satyam was rich boy, might be he was insulted deeply inside and planned for taking revenge. How could she believe that he was changed himself?

She said "Satyam I should go now. And thanks for coffee." She left the shop without his permission. But he could not stop her so he let her go and remained alone at the table for taking two more two more coffee because he had to complete the need of wine habit by replacing the coffee.

Continuously he waited for two days out of her office but she was absent and he didn't know about her leave. He could take out all information from the receptionist but he didn't want to come in focus there. And it became his daily routine to waste his time like this out of her office. His activities were suspicious for some her colleagues who were continuously observing him. Finally he saw her after 10 days. She also noticed him but tried to neglect him and went away directly. One her co-worker said her, "why does he come every day here? You know he is Satyam Desai, son of Vikram Desai. What a handsome he is! I asked him but he didn't respond."

Supriya surprised that why he was wasting his time instead of doing something. Next day she decided to meet him and told

"Why are wasting your time Satyam? Please don't give trouble more now. I already forgave you."

"Sorry Supriya, when you told me, I realized about my habits and believe I gave them all and departed from my friends also?

"It's nice but what do you want now?"

Your help ....please guides me, what I should do now? And really don't want to give trouble. But each moment is making curious to know what to do. Because I haven't did anything properly. And told me to leave what I was doing. Ok, I will not come here again if you promise me to meet in the coffee shop. Please don't get it in wrong mean."

Now there was no any doubt in her mind about his intention and the purity of mind. She knew that it was not simple thing to help him because it was good but on the same time more risky, she could have discarded him but she thought why she should reject the good work. But what she could do then it was her mistake to saw him right way. Surely now somebody should walk on this, that's why she will had to help him.

"Ok, if you want my help for good cause then I must help you. Meet me in the coffee shop tomorrow. And do one thing read some books today and tomorrow" but looking at his face she got answer that which books? "Come lets go on the book stall" she chose some books and said to pack up, meanwhile he paid the bill. She instructed him to read them carefully at time of departure. Satyam came to home and opened the box, he got a novel in the bunch, Mrityunjaya, a story of Karna, and unwillingly he started reading the novel. But he was getting the interest in reading. his parent were surprised to see him reading the philosophical novel while they were calling him for the dinner and he told that he was busy In reading. Any parent can get surprise if their child will tell them that he was busy in reading who never opened the book even during the exam. It was unexpected thing for them. In fact already they came to know about his changing behaviour.

Next day he left the house sharp at six of evening and reached to the coffee shop. Supriya also came there within few minutes. He already had given an order of coffee and some snacks but within that period Supriya was looking in his eyes.

"Even yesterday you drunk, how can you break the promise?" She said nervous mood.

"No Supriya, I haven't drunk. I was reading full night. I read Mrityunjaya." He told the truth behind his red eyes.

"What? You read this one? Ok what do learn from the book?"

We should do our work without taking pressure of future and expectation of its fruit and many things about the life. Really still kana is standing in front of me. First time I understood that books can give such type of pleasure. And I was moving far away from and calling others 'a book worms'. How stupid I was?"

"Ok nice. Now do one thing, do join your father's office from tomorrow try to help him in his busyness."

"But Supriya I don't know anything about my father's work. I have seen them. But don't know how they are doing."

"No Satyam this not true that you don't know anything , in fact you didn't tried for that to know about your fathers work, perhaps your father kept you away from that burden but on one day you have to handle this busyness, so why shouldn't you ready to learn it today? And remember this is the readymade platform for you that are better to learn. Ok..." she gave him the right path of the life. It was not great philosophy but gave him right vision to see towards the life.

"Ok. I will join the office but we will meet regularly. And tell me, what will I do if got any problem?"

"You can call me. I will guide you ok. Now satisfied?" after some discursion they left the shop. In this way they started meeting everyday in that coffee shop. He came at home and saw his father seating on the chair doing some work on laptop, said "dad I want to come with you to join the office and want to learn your work. Please let me join."

His father was shocked that how could his child tell him this thing; he could believe on his eyes whether it was the same son whom he saw last month. Suddenly this surprise turned into the pleasure that his only son wanted to learn his work. Same thing he was telling to his friends that when his son would understand his responsibility.

Everybody was engaged in activities from the morning and they all were so busy for the preparation of award function. It was very precious moment for the company. Company had won two most precious awards in the leadership of Satyam Desai. This company became very powerful within two years with the joining of Satyam as the Asst. CEO of the company. Company was declared for two awards and credit was to the hard work of workers, clean administration, social awareness, outstanding decisions, devotion of staff and most important the leadership of Satyam created the prominent position of the company. Today news paper, TV channels were showing the news about Satyam and his achievement. Surely, it was important for him because a journey of vagabond child towards a successful businessman was unbelievable to everyone. Satyam was awarded with the 'A Young Dynamic Businessman of the Year' as well as 'Businessman of the Year' and company honoured with 'Company of the Year' award. He told his story in function but willingly avoided to say about Supriya but he said which incident changed his life and suddenly he became the aware about his identity.

There Supriya was so happy to listen the news her friend has created his own existence. Today he wanted to gift her but could not understand what to gift her and he didn't want to give her that can be the reason for her anger. He planned to gift her trophy of the award.

"You are very lucky for me Supriya. You are my luck. All credits goes to you. Without your help it was impossible for me."

She smiled and said, "Thanks for that. But Satyam it's your hard work and loyalty that brought you on this position. Nature wanted to make you something and I am just the medium. It's true that I shown you the way but it was you who walked firmly after lot challenges. I am really proud of you."

Suddenly he took out something from the bag covered with golden paper. "It's for you"

"But what is it. I don't want any gift Satyam. "

"Just open it and see what it is. If you don't like then you can return it to me"

She laughed and opened it and shocked, looking at with spread eyes. She could not believe on her eyes. There was a book in her hand 'secrets of my businesses by Satyam Desai. It was the first copy of the book and still the publication was remaining.

"By the way I liked it but without your sign it is incomplete. Sir may I get autograph please?"

Satyam signed on the front page. Satyam ordered coffee and small cake to celebrate his achievement. Supriya turned the page, she got second shock, and the book was dedicated to the writer's friend, philosopher and guide-Supriya Pradhan.

"Supriya since two years we are meeting in this coffee shop, same taste we are taking every day. Today is my most precious day, whatever I am today it's only because of you. Its day for celebration, can we go for dinner" his childish words smiled Supriya "hmm. Before you speak I read it in your eyes, what you wanted to tell. Come let's go."

He opened the door of his own car, on own earning. He took her in the five star hotel. Before going to the hotel she called that she will come late and going for dinner with Satyam. Her parents also knew about their friendship. They were afraid before one year but now they also came to know about his changed behave and their good friendship.

Off course within those two years their friendship slightly changed in little love. But they could not say to each other. They could read it in each other's eyes. Satyam was afraid to loss her and waited for achieve something, he didn't know that he was fallen in love at the time when she told him the reality of his bad behaviour but he didn't know when she became his friend, philosopher and guide. And for Supriya Satyam was the son one of the richest man in the Mumbai. She was happy with his friendship only. She knew that dreams are good but not reliable. But today Satyam realized the necessity of telling her about his love for what he was waiting since one year.

"Supriya, I want to tell you something today. Actually everyone give something treat to his near and dear one but today I want something from you. You know everyone gave me gifts on my success but I don't have any interest in that. I want the gift from you." Satyam put into the confusion. She knew that nothing was there which was difficult to achieve him.

"Ok tell what do you want? After all it's your day. I will it if it will be possible for me except my pride and honour." She said him doubtfully

He started laugh very slowly and said, "Will you marry with me?"I want your company for whole life as my life partner. I really love since that moment I saw you in the hospital. I wanted tell that moment when I appreciated by my family but I wanted to be something as you told. You are one who opened my eyes and taught me like philosopher. Don't feel hesitation if you don't want to give answer now, I can wait for the whole life for you. And I will feel bad if you will say no, because you are most important me as the friend. Supriya smiled with tears fallen down on soft fair chicks. Some moments come in our life when both contrast feelings we can enjoys, pleasure and grief together.

"What do you think that I don't know what's going on in your eyes? I know everything you wanted to tell. I came to know about this on that day when you came and waited for ten days outside of my office. Since two years I am watching pure and spontaneous love in your eyes, but didn't respond you, because I didn't want to destroy your life and living such divesting life. When I came with you in coffee shop, I gabled with my own life, which could be destroy my life. But you already won me. I am always with you" she opened herself with the words as if she stored them all for this valuable day.

"Will marry with me" Satyam asked her very in eager. She replied him, "Yes I will do."

Today they decided everything but had departed unwillingly due to the time. It was ten o'clock. Satyam drop her at the home. But both could not understand what to talk with love one. But they were talking very little with the great feeling of their company. Satyam wanted to tell his parent about his love and wanted to marry with Supriya. He knew that his father loves him so much.

He told his mother but he got negative answer from mother that she wanted her brother's daughter as her daughter in law while his father had given promise to his own businessman friend for his only daughter. How could they accept any middle class girl as their daughter in law? No doubt it was against of their culture and social status which was tightly bounded with the economical threads leading them to aristocratic society. They both were against of his decision; even his father told if he had done any physical relation, then gives her some money and leaves her. What could he expect from them more than this? It was very simple for them to decide price of anything. They strictly warn him to marry with the girl that they would decide and do forget the girl, his love. He tried to convince them that he had nothing without her; even this new life was given by her. She had taken lot of efforts. He even told them that it was better to die than to forget her. But they were his parent, everyday facing such deathly challenges of the business and even they had been seen such events through their life; perhaps they had been watching such Romeos, who became normal after the marriage, the same they thought about Satyam, hence they had minded it as the business deal, instead of emotional deal.

It's the rule of the nature human goes under the control of ego with increasing power(money), experience and age increase; some exceptions always there but Mr. Desai was fitted himself into the rule. Next day he called to Rakesh Pradhan, a very middleclass person, who didn't know why he was called by Desai. He told to do the marriage of Supriya as possible as early, promised to do all the expense what they wanted. Mr. Pradhan thought he was giving him help to show his gratitude of his daughter's efforts to improve his son. But suddenly Mr. Desai told all the things told by his son about their love. Finally, Mr. Desai came on his aptitude and   forewarn him to do the police case or do the criminal act if he found his daughter again with the Satyam. What could do the poor man in this condition, so he accepted his proposal; no one would face such egoistic person. So Rakesh Pradhan took wise and fair decision to do marriage of his daughter. But what he did know what was in the mind of future.

Here at home Supriya clearly rejected the matte of marriage with anyone, opened the matter of her love with Satyam and told both of their decision of the marriage. But her father didn't want to listen, as he came to know before. She tried to convince but her father make confused that he was going to marry with his maternal uncle's daughter and he was only playing with her. However she could not believe when he knew everything about Satyam but she could not discard her father's words.

There Mr. Desai started playing a mind game with the Satyam. It was the matter of his prestige and social status. Within two days he planned for Satyam. He decided to do the marriage of Supriya in absence of Satyam. He called Satyam and told him to be ready for the business summit within an hour. Satyam was told in the meeting that he would be the leader of the team and should go to Indonesia for business summit, to learn more advance technology in building construction and civil engineering for the 15 days. Unfortunately all team were ready to go. He had only half an hour to move, it was difficult to inform her within this time. Mr. Desai exchanged his personal mobile with company's mobile due to he could not contact with Supriya. Mr. Pradhan deliberately had broken her mobile by fallen down from second floor. She believed that the news given by her father wasn't more reliable about his marriage so she made her mind up to meet Satyam and taken out the fact behind her father's statement. But she flabbergasted while watchman messaged her that he didn't want to encounter her which was mind-boggling for her. She returned with snuffle and told her father to make preparation for the marriage as they wished, but inner her mind knew that she can't live without him.

Early in the morning, everybody was searching to Satyam on airport to receive him. He gave a responsibility to his on senior person to submit the report if the summit. He directly went out from the airport, where could he go; of course to meet Supriya. From 15 days he had not any contact with the Supriya but today he couldn't stop himself. During that summit he met many businessmen who founded their companies on their own will. And he had planned to start his own company. Many people were familiar with his name, they agreed to help him. So he decided to start his own small business with Supriya. And he believed that if would with him, he can anything. Supriya was his fortune and everything happened fine with arrival in his life.

He reached at her house, what he saw? There was nice decoration around her house. Everyone was happy. He thought that it was some ones marriage but he saw Mr. Pradhan was doing the work and making some preparation, engaged in some activities of the marriage, Satyam could not understand what the matter was. but he didn't wasted much time and asked to one relative person who informed him that it was Supriya's marriage ceremony, he was remain only to cry but what to do. He decides to meet Supriya but on the same moment Mr. Pradhan saw him and stopped him and spelt him out form the place. He could not understand how could she do this with him like this? He went out form there in anger.

It was time of evening all were engage in the groundwork of pre marriage ceremony. Suddenly someone come out with shouting, all women were started crying. Nobody had any idea what was happened actually, while everything was fine till the moment. Within a few moments ambulance came with warning distress signal sound. Everyone was shocked to the Supriya on the stretcher, yes it was Supriya faint down in her restroom, and found in half dead condition. She got the news that Satyam came at her home and her family members were not allowed him to meet her therefore she called him but as usual his mobile was switch off finally she called at home. Here she was the problem, their housekeeper received the call and informed her that everyone was in the hospital and the reason was very serious. While Satyam left her house, on the way he had a dangerous accident at morning, when he came from Indonesia. Now she was completely fallen down and what to do could not understand. There was no any use of live this life so she has taken the poison slept very silently.

Mr. Vikram Desai was waiting outside of the ward, what doctors would the news, so much worried. Supriya and Satyam both were admitted in the same ward of emergency. Mr. Desai noticed that in front of him Mr. Pradhan and his family was also seating in the same pain. Today he empathized when we stand in front of the God to beg, each one is equal, same; no rich, no poor.

Suddenly, doctors came out and informed that they could not save Supriya after hard trials. On the same time Mr. Desai got news that doctors were fail doing the operation of Satyam. They could not understand what to say about Satyam.

Mr. Desai was looking towards all of them as if begging for the repentance. Only because of his small decision, how many people were suffered. After all, Supriya and Satyam would meet in the heaven, but what about the people on the earth. What was wrong in the desire of Mr. Desai? What was wrong in the love between Supriya and Satyam?

What would have happened if they got married? Did social calamity come? Would world finish? Nothing was possible. These are questions only to convince the mind. But how can we blame to the people when nature plays its game with us. No doubt we are the puppets in the hands of fortune.

Same moody nature had finished its game and put both puppets in the box.

***

7

I Am Sorry....

"Radha ! Radha!! How much I have to search you girl. Why are seating here and why are you crying? What does happen with my dude?" Meena wondered to saw Radha. Who were always strict and stuff in any critical condition.

"Nothing is happened but something feeling pain in heart. You know this study makes me so tired." Radha stopped and started watching towards city roads beyond the window. Hundred of vehicles were passing on it but a single mind was still keeping watch on vehicles.

"I know what your problem is. But Radha we have to forget all the things. I mean don't think more about her more. In fact nobody is unknown about your good friendship. And now you are alone. But everyone has to go but I know it was unfortunate incident with her, she left us. And we should not forget this that life doesn't stop for anyone.

"But she dint commit suicide. It was perfect murder and what about Rohit? He killed her Meena." Radha answered.

"Ok! Let it go! Shall we go for tea? You will feel better. Come on now." Meena taken her hand and both started walking towards the canteen.

Radha and Meena were good friends; actually Kavita was also with them. Kavita was a beautiful and talent girl from Ahamadnagar. All three were belonged from various parts of the Maharashtra. Before two days Kavita were married and she has committed suicide in her house everyone was shocked to listen the news of her death. But the surprising thing was that no one felt need to know the reason behind her death. Here Radha was in the pain due to their good and nice friendship which was known to each one even to their family members also. She hurt more than anyone in her family.

Radha was nearest and dearest one to the Kavita so both was very close very close to each other's secrets. But Meena just shifted to Radha's room for her company Radha was very different type of girl. Quit as tomboy, didn't feel any emotion. Rarely could she find out crying and weeping to only Kavita; not to anyone. On the contrary Kavita was the girl of emotions and sensitive thoughts in the college. And always ready to pardon for others mistakes. Frequently Radha was committing mistakes and Kavita would say sorry for her mistake. It was like the tradition in their room. Radha was absolutely against of the love and such heartily emotions. But she came to know about Kavita's love affair with one boy of the college. No need of any predictor to say whether Radha would be known about her love one. In fact she told her everything about him to the Radha. Radha was making always fun about her love story. But Kavita didn't mind it and always saying that she would complete her love story one day but where she did know what game will future play in her life.

Her friend's death was making melancholic and depressed her each moments. Meena ordered tea and some snacks on the same tea stall Radha and Kavita taking every day. That was there regular routine to go for tea, and it's important to make yourself free and relax while you have a tension.

"Would you like to eat something? You haven't taken anything from two days. Let's done thing, today we should go out for dinner" Meena suggested her. Suddenly Raghu uncle came there. Both were shocked.

"How are you beta? What's about your study? I know how education becomes so difficult now days. Aren't you feeling better? " Raghu kaka was owner of canteen and running inn for all girls students who was taking great care of all girls like his own daughters. He knew about the real problem of Radha little bit but still he wanted to make good atmosphere. It was his skill to change the mood of any person and he had great knowledge of human tendency. And surprising thing was that hardly he had completed his primary school.

"Yes uncle I am fine. Today just I came from village. I will come for dinner tonight." Radha informed him.

"Ok daughter. Please take care of your health.

See!! You're your tea came. Enjoy it." Raghu kaka said and them to enjoy the tea. Raghu kaka was always keeping watch on the girls of college while they were coming in his canteen. If he found anything wrong about the girl, tries to advise her to keep distance from it due to his good nature. Many people were unknown about the death of Kavita. It wasn't shocking for them. Might be some were known about her death but this was not good news for them.

After taking tea Meena advised Radha to go in market for shopping; it could be only the reason to take out Radha from that dark room of the hostel. Girls are fonder of shopping and market. Meena said her to buy something. So they started walking towards the market. Both were walking on the road while Radha was only giving the reply, like 'yes or No' Radha had only taking her to let her forget about the Kavita. She noticed about the Radha while walking on the way that Radha was turned into panic to remember about the Kavita and her bargaining with the shopkeepers for the price of the things.

After that they both returned to the hostel and prepared to go for dinner. Radha took dinner but little than she required. Anyone could read her pale face how she was in the tension and her nervous mind. Meena was seating in the chair and reading the book preparing for exam in the room after dinner.

Radha broke that Satanic silence," Meena, what is love? Do you know about it something? And really anyone can be mad to do anything for their love." Meena was surprised to listen what she was talking about. But she felt good at least she started talking on such topics.

"Yes I listen it and am feeling also. Many stories

I listened about it but one thing tell me miss karate, why are you asking this today? Haven't you fallen in love?" asked Meena.

"No. I can't do it but I am so afraid about it. Felt guilty about this. Meena I want to tell you something about Kavita's death." Radha said.

Meena kept her book aside folded her hand. "Radha if any problem is there then please tell me. I am with you." Meena assured her. Meena's motions were indicating her readiness to listen Radha's words about Kavita. Radha started o talk about Kavita.

"Meena, it is the story of that time when we all were newly admitted in the college. We introduced at the first time and really she was fantastic girl, became my best friend within few days. I don't what was the relation that made us good friends. Everyone knew about our friendship. Once we went for Garba festival. She was really good dancer and very fond of dance in such festival. That day we came in the contact with our one senior, Rahul. Rahul was from Gujarat. He was very nice in study. He was in the last year that time. He attracted towards Kavita and she was also towards Rahul. She wanted to learn Guajarati Garba from Rahul. He was good Garba dancer. So she did friendship with him. Within those nine days they both come together and I noticed it about their behaviour.

"She also said me about that. Rahul was good boy but I didn't like their friendship and especially illegal relation between them. I think boys are really selfish, use anyone for their personal advantages. They like only to play with us. They only want to enjoy with us. Use us for their lust.

After them both started to meet each other, dating each other. At first few days they had some fear but after getting it habited, they were meeting openly without caring anyone. I saw some changes in Kalpana and she was living in her own world. She completely neglected to the study. She was really happy but I didn't like how she was living. I had fear many times about her. It was I who wanted something good for her. I hadn't any jealous about her but lot of care. I gave many warnings her but she didn't listen my words.

On the other side Rahul was the son of typical Guajarati businessman who always dealt with money. His father was really so miser. Rahul was the person of ego of money and he was always had bad behaviour with other boys but he was in love with Kavita. And for my friend I started to find out more information about Rahul and his past life, what he did at last year. And really I was correct about his past. Every year he changed his girlfriend and deceiving everyone. And that year he selected Kavita. I was completely confused what to do with that thing because she wasn't in the mood to understand my words. Even four times she had quarrelled with me on this topic. She was completely unknown about coming quandary. Believe me Meena I just wanted to save her. My intention was really pure." Radha started crying after these words. It is too difficult to stop in such condition.

"Then what did happened Radha?" now Meena wanted to know about that incident that came like the climax in their life. "Means did Rahul deceive her and pushed her in the mouth of death?" she asked.

"No Meena! He didn't. When I told her that Rahul is not good boy, she fought with and said many things. Even she warned me to destroy. I was completely unbearable what to do. She challenged me to complete her love in any condition. That time I came to understand that she was following in the love of that boy. She was going out of my hands. I had fear about the result of their affair and finally that happened what fear I had.

One day her brother came to the college to meet her, he had something another work in the city, so just casually he came here to meet her. Actually as his sisters friend he call me his second sister. We have good communication. On the same time she had gone with Rahul for movie outside. I said that she had lecture. I we both went to canteen for tea. How I did know about them we were just taking tea suddenly Rahul and Kavita came in canteen in wrong manner. They didn't know about his presence in the canteen. He saw them in very miserable condition. her family came to know all their all matter and here she doubted on me that I told her family about her brother's arrival. I explained her lot times about that.

After that problematic situation her family was became serious about their status in the society. So they decided her marriage and without her approval they fixed her marriage. I talked on the topic and try to convince for marriage because her family members were forcing me to talk about the matter.

It is the thing of one day when I was seating on the chair and preparing for the exam. She had not any worry about the study so she was calm and lost in her problem. I could understand her problem but what I could do for that. Suddenly she went for the washroom. I heard her omitting sound from washroom. I saw her vomiting in the basin when I reached there within moment. I thought It was casual due to food poisoning but I came to know that she was pregnant while we both went that evening for normal check up to the doctor. They said that she was pregnant and had very critical condition about the health. I was in fear what to do about her condition and wanted for abortion but doctors were not ready to do without her parent's consultation and permission. I took my one relative to the doctor for more help. I knew that she would kill her in that condition. here I wanted to save her life; on other hand she was not ready for the abortion. She believed that her family is searching for right choice but if they would came to know about her pregnancy they would have allow for their marriage but that innocent baby never known that how her family would allow that stupid thing. she thought will become happy to listen that news and they both would tell all the things to their both families. I wanted to meet Rahul and wanted to clear that matter and I had know what his reaction on that was. So I went to meet him.

As I expected he was also more worried about that thing. He said sorry for that to me but what was the use of that his sorry while he did great loss of that innocent child. I told him the condition because pregnancy is like the curse for any pre-marital woman. Finally with the help of my uncle I made him ready successfully for the marriage. At last I decided to tell her brother about that condition. It was great calamity for me to explain that thing in front of her brother. At first he was became mad to kill Rahul who destroyed her sister's life but when I realized him that Kavita was responsible somewhere about that condition. Still he rejected that and said that his family will never accept this. But he became ready to take the responsibility of abortion what we did against of her wish." Radha became silent after these words. As if did crime.

"What did happen then next? If Rahul was ready for marriage then why didn't they eloped? How her marriage was fixed to another one." Meena wanted to know about her.

"Yes he told me that he would marry with Kavita but he ran away to his village I hadn't any contact with him. I got the news that he had also done marriage. I dint know how he behaved like this. And her family was also unknown about that. Finally, her marriage was fixed with one boy. On that day she called me and urgently wanted to meet.

She told me how much she loved him. Infect they had decided to do love marriage. but then it was impossible for both of them because I destroyed their plan. They wanted to give legal name for their relation but situation made that disturbed. To also her last word is sounding, she said, "Radha I know you are really worried for me but I want to live with Rahul. You can't understand our love. We really love each other. I know you don't believe in love but remember one day you will believe and I will make you believe. Radha I can't live without Rohit. Our love is true. But we will meet in heaven.

Meena I knew about her death but yet could not do anything for that. I was unable to do anything for that. I could save her life If I helped her that day. After only two days I got the news that she committed suicide and you know on the same day Rohit also committed suicide." Radha started crying.

"What? Rohit also died on the same day?" Meena got shocked.

"Yes. My dear both had completed their promises. They both taught me about love. She used to say about love that they would complete their love in the heaven. But here it became incomplete. Therefore they both went in another world to make it complete. Radha became quite. Meena and Radha both were looking stars as Kavita and Rahul both were looking at them telling them about their incomplete love in this mortal world.

***

8

Slap

Vehicles are being parked and people started to come in the building. Morning time is really good and especially you can enjoy it in Aurangabad more. As we know that it is the historical city and hence people come here to such sign of the history. It is Famous as the city of 52 gates. But Mahesh didn't know about the city more. First time came in the city from the home to see what happened of his life. It was the turning point of his life when life will write new chapter of his life.

High court of the Aurangabad is one of the busiest places in Aurangabad where people come to decide their life and related matters. Murder, corruption, deceiving and so hundreds of cases force people to enter here. But Mahesh came here with different matter in this polished building when people come to clean their matters.

Mahesh, a young graduate boy just started a job of teaching in a private school. Well educated personality also had kind heart and generous mind. Mahesh was the first boy graduated from university of his village. So the value of Mahesh was quite great in the eyes of other peasants. There were no such facilities available in his village. He always ready to help others as if it was his nature and would get the pleasure from. Peasants also would like to tell him any work of district or Tahsil related due to his good communication and good connection with the people. He never discarded anyone.

He born in middle class family and by birth he was good in study. Everybody was telling that one day he will be on the good position. And it was his nature which was carrying him in the mind of young generation also as if one inspiration.

Everybody knew about this struggling boy how he had taken the struggles for the family and the education. It was not simple for him when he had completed his university education though his family condition was not so good. His ideal qualities kept him always on the on the others lips. He ensured about to change his life very soon. He had the knowledge about his parent's expectations about his life. It didn't mean that his parents had unlimited expectations from him. But they wanted that their child should be happy whatever he will get in his life. What does parent want more than that?

When he was in the college never glanced at girls even. In fact it was very easy for him to catch anyone's attraction due to his handsome personality. Many girls proposed him but this moralistic boy believed on marriage love. He often says that he would not distribute his love like prashad to anyone. Once he told beautiful words to girls when she proposed him in the college, "madam my love is not the gad's prashad that can be distribute to anywhere. Sorry madam I can appreciate your love but I am not deserve for it. I can't accept. I will give everything to my wife only."

On that one this friends were teasing him many times. But what could he explain? He was just smiling on their words. He wanted to enjoy the life and the love with his wife only. He believed on the sacrifice for her. He says that why shouldn't he sacrifice for her while she would sacrifice for him.

His thoughts about marriage were really fantastic. He learnt cooking and others things also to impress his future wife. He was always telling about the marriage that the incarnation of the man's qualities in woman and woman's qualities in man as well as the arising in their mind and increasing the love for each other is a marriage. He would always disgust to see the love affairs of his friends, saying them that they were deceiving their parents.

In this way he had completed his college education and as he had completed college, he joined on school for teaching. He desired to be the teacher since his childhood and hi was 'sir' for his relatives and family members as well as friends.

As he got good job family members started to find out well bride for him. Silently he was also ready for the marriage after all he was child of his parent to complete their wish of his marriage. So felt the right time to complete their wish. But from the deep of heart he was not ready for marriage before making his career but when all convinced him then how could he opposed?

His family wanted the girls to look after family member and Mahesh well. Educated, good looking girl they wanted for their lovely son. They expected that his wife should help him in his all work related the school.]

As said by his parents they called Mahesh to choose out a girl among many bio-data and photos came to them. Mahesh saw all girls but his mind and eyes fixed on one picture as if she was made for him only. And her image was waiting for his sight to catch. Mahesh chose the image and handed to his mother to show his readiness towards. His mother understood all what wanted to say.

What was after that? His parents decided to complete all further procedure of rituals and be proceeding for this. They also liked his choice.

The girls were in his relation. She was working as nurse in the hospital. They listened many things about her but were relax by saying blood relation with the family. After fifteen days when she had a holiday, they decided wedding and engagement program. Mahesh was very happy to saw her first time. He heartily liked her simplicity, sincere behavior and beautiful look attracted him towards her. Full day he was just looking to her. And how can anyone left his sight, all noticed his eyes and therefore many had advised him in teasing manner to meet her in alone and complete his desire. But Mahesh denied the idea. Because he knew that she was coming in his life. Then why does meet to her in alone? He fell in love with first sight and he wanted to feel it.

He had proud that his future wife had taken the education related to the medical field and working as the nurse in hospital far away from the house. Actually he had the respect for the field and related people whenever he was looking towards them due to their serving nature to the society. Society is always blessing them heartily, for their responsible service. And therefore he had been feeling respect for his wife also.

After his wedding he came to know her name was Riya. A well educated and knowledge girl. Her father was respective fellow in the village. He wanted that his daughter should take more education and learns more than any other child in the village and should stand upon her legs independently. He did that. Riya didn't like village due to its illiterate people, unclean porches, dust, rustic and unmannered because she grew in the city light area. In fact she didn't get time to know her village, to understand the people, their emotions, feeling and their generous hearts. She was practical woman who never care for anyone's mind. Looking towards the fallen blind man she said that he must had done some sins in his last birth so he is suffering from such problem, instead to help that man. She thought about others very practically and critically. It was the test of their fate, family to bring them together to make a lovely family and make their marriage successful.

After many conditions she responded positively for the marriage. Here Mahesh was very happy after got the news. But now his mind was not ready to wait more for her. Patience reached its heights; he wanted to talk with her. Wanted to tell her about him and wanted to listen about her life and emotions. Sometime he was just thinking about her and only was thinking about her, every where he was looking to her. Simply he was mad in her love. He started to dream of Riya, his future wife.

Somehow, after many hesitations he got her mobile number while his friends were asking him whether they were talking to her or not, what they were talking and he replied them 'no'. Now his friends were started teaching him about woman, how to attract her attention and how to make her aware about him and his love for her. First time he called her to say 'Good morning!!' but how much afraid he was!!As if he had seen dangerous thing in the dark room of the ancient house. That time he felt that he had heart, its pulse and beats, But with uttered voice, "hi... good morning. I am Mahesh here.' It's true whether he is king or any sultan, turn dumb and deaf when the first time comes to express emotion to the beloved. Then how can Mahesh be exception for the universal truth? Mahesh started talking with her but on the other side she was trying to show her embarrass nature to him and towards his romantic chatting as if only she was only completing the formalities. There was no way for her except talking to him. Mahesh knew that she is the nurse and having many works in the hospital, not teacher like him.

In few days as a tradition they went to select the clothes for marriage, shopping. Mahesh and Riya were seated beside each other for selecting the clothes Mahesh was looking each sari very carefully. He was taking lot interest in selection. Red, yellow, blues he just trying to choose the sari for her. Which will be more attractive or better look her. These all things he was looking in the sari, what one woman look into. Mahesh knew that this memorable event never come in his life again. Marriage is the event which never come back in the life, it perform once in the life. Most important he got the girl as he wanted as his life partner.

In that all were looking towards the Mahesh and silently making the jokes and started laugh at him whenever he was looking sari very carefully. 'See how he is excited about this than his wife. Ha ha!!!!" and at same time his friends were much surprised about Riya and her less interest in such activities. His friends came to know that she was only physically present in the program. She was not showing any interest in this. All were looking this very easily.

Riya took all that selected by Mahesh without saying any word, doubt, or never had any resistance to his choice. But Mahesh didn't get himself nervous from the situation. In fact he thought that she accepted his choice. But got shocked when he asked her to select his clothes for him and she gave unexpected reply to his innocent demand.

"See, now you choose my clothes. Which shirt will suit me? I want to know your choice for me. Come... let's check."

"But how can I know your choice. I don't have any sense about clothes. Please you can take what you want. I don't mind it. You can take anything you want for you. And finish it as early as possible. I am getting bore here. Please do it fast and let me go." Everyone was shock to listen this answer. How could she use such language in front of all relatives? With whom she was talking and how, with her future husband Mahesh. Mahesh was completely confused on the unrelated matter of the cloth shop. In fact for whole evening he was sank in his deep thoughts. He came to know that they were taking more time for such quick program than usual so they started it to do fast and very simply.

He didn't want to make any issue of such very normal matter. Even he requested and convinced to his family members to forget the matter whatever happened between them. Hurriedly they completed the rituals and formalities and came to home. There was pleasure on each face with the completed job but no need to who face was not so happy with the incident. He had no problem what she said but his problem was something different, related with something another matter.

'Why she said this in front of all. There was no need to tell everyone. If really she was getting bore then she could told to me. May be in her view I can't understand to her and unable to know her. Definitely she was in some problem neither how could she talk like this to me. I know her very at least she is not like this to use such rough and tough language with me."

Now what to say when this person is thinking like this. We know that when love headed upon one's head then he or she became complete blind and we just forget to accept reality and don't want to see the real world and to make our brain foolish while he is the logical thinker. And here only this man does it very effectively and perfectly. Only he can do not any anyone. Still this man wanted to tell her sorry for what happened in this shop. He took out his mobile form the pocket. As soon as bell rang, she received the phone. He thanked to the god while she receive the phone. It was Riya, his dream girl and future queen.

"Hello Riya, good evening! How are you? Do not feeling well" said Mahesh as if he knew her problem.

"Ya I am feeling better but Mahesh I am really sorry what I did in the shop. I am really sorry for that." Riya was trying to clean up her side.

"It's ok. Why are you thinking this? Leave the matter. Actually I was wrong. I should have known that you have already lot of tensions and many problems. And in that you were getting bore which is simply natural for anyone and most important; you were not comfortable in that situation"Mahesh was trying to understand her and showing purposefully his good nature t her. But what reacted was also surprising to him again.

"Thank you so much Mahesh. How sweet you are. In fact I was in so much tension that what you will think about me. May be my reaction made annoyed. But you are so nice. By the way I have some important work. Bye." Riya reacted very practically to his words. Even she had no care about his call.

"But Riya want to talk with you. "Said Mahesh

"Ok but now I have some work. By the way I will call you back when I will get free" said Riya very simply to him.

In fact he was disappointed by her action but hopped better with her love magical words. Next moment he was happy to think about promise to cal him back. It was making to full him while after two days also she had no any reply even for him. And not even trying to make nay contact. Sure you are so much busy but you are not as much engaged that cannot get a time to talk with your love. Hence his patience had broken down and he wanted to get reason why she didn't want to talk with him. Anxiously he called her when had no any reply on the third day passed. He was really angry with Riya and wanted to say this so he went into attic. But she was not receiving his calls. Now he came to know that she was trying to neglect his call and not wanted to speak with him. She was not giving any response to him. He didn't know what to do now. Then finally he decided to reach at workplace and let her asks the questions why she was not giving any response. Was the work important than him. And morally for him it was the right to ask such question her future becoming husband. But while his dearest friend listen this; he stopped him to do so very anxiously without taking any patience.

"Mahesh your wife is working in the hospital and may she had lot work any she had no really time to make you call. And my dear if you there to ask her such stormy questions, maybe she would mislead you in different manner that haven't you expected. She will think that you have doubts about her work and her moral character. This action would indicate your wrong path."

Mahesh came to know that his friend was telling him with correct suggestion. He was convinced Mahesh with his icy words. He was started waiting again for the call. But when he noticed about the date of marriage was coming near, he became so happy.

He started dreaming with his future wife, started to decorating romantic scenes about Riya what they would do after marriage. He was taking each and every care about marriage ceremony. And most interesting this was that he had started to search the best place for honeymoon in the state, even started discursion with the manager about what facilities, their rates and care they take for.

She would not get time to think on such matters so all arrangement was done by him. On the same he cared about her ambition, she should not feel anything improper. Again was thinking about her health and her problems. As if she had all problems at her workplace. Meanwhile he received her some countable calls as only she had completed formality because nobody should say her that how she was not behaving well. Still he was happy to think about his wife that she was working in the hospital and gives more importance to the work than anything. Although he believed on the idea 'work is worship' what he was teaching into the class to his disciple.

Finally the most awaiting event came in his life which was eagerly awaited by all, marriage day of both. No doubt the marriage is not only the event only it's a bond of two families. Mostly everyone becomes happy and energetic in this. Most memorable moment of the person's in his life. We enjoy it like on festival. Form the morning everyone was so happy and in good mood as if never did before that. His uncles, aunts, cousins, sisters, friends and all relatives were gathered together very happily. Rarely the day comes in the life of human being when all celebrated the day together by forgetting the all type of revenges and disputes. All the preparations of ceremony had completed by all the responsible people in the village.

Now all were ready to welcome the boy –'dulha' of the day and his horse march called – 'barat'. Friends and relatives were lot engage in the marriage as if they didn't wanted to finish it with quartz. So sometimes they had to push many dancing boys on the disk jockey (do) foreword and protested their emotions. DJ, band, new clothes, celebration, work of friends etc all was feeling him prince today. This all scenario made him very happy. It was his wish and desires that he wanted before.

Panditaji started hi enchanting and hymn of marriage. When boy and his bridegroom came on the stage, surely he was looking like a king and people were being seated in his royal court. How beautiful it was. So sweet and memorable, Even Mahesh could not understand when panditji had completed it and when it was over; he just was sank into the dreams of his future life and hypnotized with married life. Now today happiest man was Mahesh. All the rituals and costumes were over and completed. Socially and legally they became husband and wife. They completed Photo session and then blessing of elders and lastly the 'saptpadi' and most important the round around the fire. And finally it was completed. Now Mahesh was not ready to wait for Riya. Silently he was waiting for her. He could not understand how much and how many he should talk with her. As the tradition we know her father took her with him after two days to her mother house. All relatives and friends were congratulated him and lastly with good blessing they all take of farewell form them and left them alone. And then he engaged himself in remain works in house.

As soon as Mahesh just completed his lunch and washed hands, postman came on the door and called his father's name after ten days of his marriage. Actually postman knew him very due to his helping nature. Many times he has been helping to his work. He serves one envelope in his hand and after some formal talking went away. Mahesh could not understand what was it? With confused mind he opened the packet and started reading. No sooner he finished reading than fallen down on the floor. But try to balanced somehow. As if someone stabbed him very savagely. His mother and neighbors came there and wanted to know what had happened with him. All were asking to him but he was not telling anything and another problem was there was no one who could know English. Mahesh became unconscious to talk anything, continuously was looking only towards the packet. But somehow he recovered by people, he just went away without the word. And nobody was able to understand what to say. No any topic to talk on the happened event. All were started their logics about.

Mahesh took out mobile and called to Riya, "hello Riya. Mahesh is here. I want to talk with you."

"I know what you will talk. I think you got it today. Lovely present "said Riya harmlessly

"Riya what happened? Why are you doing this? Had I done any mistake? Why are you troubling me this way?"Mahesh started crying like small child and why not? After all he had played like small child.

"Mahesh. Don't be angrier. No need to be highly embarrassed. Don't be silly now please. Actually you should come to know this before that. I don't love you, Mahesh and now listened calmly. I already wanted to marry with Sameer, whom I love. But my father was not agreeing with my decision with this and they forced me to marry you. My father already declared that he will not give me single penny of property if I marry with him. So I agree to marry you and before that my condition to give me half property. And as my father promised, gave me half of the property just before two days of our marriage. And therefore I had to marry you. There was no option for me. In fact I can't live with you or without Sameer. He can't live without me, either he will suicide. And I wanted to save both my father and my love" Riya explained her side very logically for Mahesh.

"Riya I can't live without you. And what you did. For saving your father and love you killed me simply. No I can't leave you. You are my wife and I will not give you any divorce. I can't accept this letter" Mahesh requesting to the Riya.

"No need be so much emotional Mr. Mukes.

Whether you will give it or not this is not matter. We will see this into the court. Just check the date and be ready to attend the court. We will meet there on given date.bye!!!"

Loud bell of courtroom wand rung and he went into the court. This bell was suggesting him to come in reality and say what decision should take for the life now. Many useless and baseless charges applied on Mahesh by Riya In courtroom. What decision would court take that was another matter but now just Mahesh got strong slap by his fortune and Riya.

He had been thinking about his love story which was again said as an incomplete one. His friends were right or he doesn't know but the game was very powerful. One thing was sure about him, he will never love again in his life. And its pray to god not to make any new Mahesh in front of me.

***

9

Waiting for love

Everyone was in hurry from early in morning. Everyone was trying to do his work properly without fail. This day was looking like celebration in the village therefore whole school is decorated. Yes, there was a celebration of the school. School plays most important role in our life. That always has new incarnation in the life. School is like mother who saw Number of people who made their currier in the same ground and premises. There is always importance of the school in every one's life. We have many memories about school and about our teachers. Therefore today is the same celebration. Anandpur is a beautiful village which has new tradition to enjoy and celebrate the exam. Today there was farewell function of SSC students. And another most important event is to congratulate the students who stood with good marks in last exam. And as tradition we have to call someone who can inspire to student and motivate them for their best future. And such person should also have some success story for the students which will motivate them to run towards their success. It's true that when you have something, people run behind you for your bless and when you don't have anything no one will understand you anyhow.

Near about all preparation had done. Student started to come in the premises and school ground/. Everyone was so much happy to see such atmosphere in the school. All teachers and students were engaged in their selected words. And most important student and teacher are happy. Because the special guest call for the program is very important person. There is curiosity to know him and how he became a successful IAS officer. And why they don't have such emotional attachment about him. After all he is also the domicile of the same village. After 10 years he is coming to this village and as the special guest in the same village, where from he was thrown out with lot of insult. How can anyone build his career after many accidents in the life? And it's really difficult. To us that to build career after many calamities. We can't say which moment will bring what to us.

From last three years whole village has been fascinated with name, Raghav Mohite, IAS, Who is known as one of the most decorated officers in Maharashtra government. Students wanted to hear his success stories and most important he hadn't forgotten his village. But today he is coming to his village then there is most attraction in students.

All are waiting for Raghav sir. It's morning time, 10 o'clock. All are seated in the programme's place. All teachers and students are seated. In one safe corner some retired teachers are seated to see Raghav. Who were teaching to him? Who are well known about Raghav? They are invited because they knew more about Raghav, about his family background but especially they came to see Raghav, the boy who they beat more and expelled from the school for under the pressure of sarpanch and panchayat. At least they wanted to say sorry for what they did with him.

Suddenly Raghav wakeup in the car, he just slept down in the morning while travelling in the car due to the meeting he attended in ministry last late night. He is looking towards the road and tried to tress the exact location where they are. Form early morning they left the city for going his village.

"How far it is again Mahesh?" Raghav asked his young driver

"Sir, only 30 kilometres are remaining. It will take one hour" he informed him.

"Sir, why did you go there? So far it is. And you don't have such time to pass. You are government officer." Informal talking made light on Raghav's face.

"Mahesh, it's my village and you know how much we are connected with our village. You can't forget some things in your life. "Changing expressions on Raghav's face are telling something to Mahesh.

"Sir, I am with you from two years. I know about you very well. You are completely dedicated for the work. But your face is telling something special. That I haven't seen ever. Hundred percent there is something very special in your life. If don't mind. I want to listen about your childhood."Mahesh asked him about his life story.

"Ohhh no nothing is special like this, dear. Just my family left the village and me too. Any couldn't go back to there. But relatives are there. It's my native place and you know how much we eager to go there where our roots are connected." Raghav simply avoided his story for Mahesh. After all he is IAS officer and have sense what to say and to whom.

But still he could not avoid himself and his mind which was waiting for someone since last ten years. How can he forget that all? It was turning point of his life. And when something enormous you have, it can't be forget. Yes. Radha is glittering name in the life of Raghav, who he loves a lot. His love story start with the name and end with this name. Last ten he just passed away by loving this name. Suddenly that small cute face came in front of his eyes when he raised his left hand where the letter is written 'R'.

He saw her first time when he took admission in 5th standard. Because. There were two different primary schools separated for girls and boys. And he took admission for the high school where first time he saw Radha, A beautiful and cute girl. Her smile was so cute and for the whole day he watched her face only. And happily said to all about his first day how it was fantastic.

That time he didn't know about her and such felling of love and liking etc. At least that much knowledge he had not at that time. So he could explain exactly what it was. And then everyday he was just looking to her. The boy who was doing many dramas to avoid the school now the first boy entered in to school. In fact it was not less than magic for his family. Much time was beaten by the teachers but that was not matter for him. He could bear all the things for her. There was no such feeling about career and life etc and however, what was the age to think about such things. He would get any to see her.

After few days they were divided in divisions. Unfortunately he put in 'B' division and she was in a division. Now, what to do with the condition? He became angry with teachers and school management but why especially he didn't know. But when teacher was allotted to the class, Mr. Bairagi was there class teacher, who was quit energetic and so awesome teacher. His first impression attracted to the Raghav. What great his speaking style. And he tried to understand the student. However, many had fear that what type of teacher they will get for their class because they had listened many things about the school. How teachers beat to students very mercilessly. But he believe that the teacher is not a demon to beat the student, he just want to make student as his duty.

Mr Bairagi was very famous teacher among the students because he was always standing in favour of student. Even any student made mistake he wasn't just telling him his mistake but tries to improve that.

In the course of time Raghav became his favourite student in the class and so he was telling many things to Raghav. It was good chance to Raghav always to in 'A' division for asking the questions when Bairagi sir was in that class. No need to say his pure intension to usually go into the class.

He got many friends in the class whom he did not know before that. His village was not so big but at least it had twenty thousand populations. Therefore it was very easy to know everyone by his name. Even postman can find anyone by his nick name only. Friends are really important for us because they are not related to our family and they understand our feeling easily. That's same was with Raghav. He got many friends in his school still them he recalls.

Raghav, Manish, Ramesh, Shyam, Kanhaiya , Deepak, Rakesh, Prashant etc were always stay together but they were not only friends it was unity for each other. They had all secrets of each other but never broke out anywhere. And it was very difficult to leave Raghav's movement. One day all friend caught him and asked that why he looked always to Radha. He could not say anything. But when all started laughing to him and promise him that they will always in his support him in any condition. They forced him many times to propose her. But it was not possible for him. Even he had not allowed to anyone to tell her about.

Radha was daughter of Sampat savant, sarpanch of the village. He was very angry and so mad person. Nobody liked him but still everyone had fear about him. He was like don of the village. He was sarpanch because he was troubling to all anyhow and always move in cross to anyone. So it was better to members to make him sarpanch to do something in the village. He had proud on his hereditary. And to love on such person's daughter was daring task. But still his friends were ready to take risk. But Raghav knew that it was not simple. Even he knew that Radha also was looking at him.

Raghav was completely fascinated with Radha. Even many times he was writing her name on benches and tries to attach it with his name. And in this way the day came when they had to face the board exam. It was very sad moment for Raghav to celebrate because he didn't know what will happen in the future. His sad face was not familiar to anyone and so it was caught easily by Bairagi sir. He called him and asked the reason for.

"Sir, actually I am unhappy to leave this school. And I will miss teachers like you. I know sir after that we will not meet again. I miss you all sir."

"Raghav this is your school and we are not going anywhere it's your village and you came here anytime without any restrictions. What are you talking my child? I wish that my student will do something grand and I should proud on my students."Bairagi sir said with hope which was not formal speech.

Raghav was just looking towards Radha. He noticed that she also was looking at him as if she wanted to say something but if it was just formality then. Raghav could tell anything to her. And this way it finished with the function. Now he focussed on the words told by his favourite teacher. He knew that it was time to take action not for emotional act. So he focussed on study.

Raghav and his friends gave exam very carefully. No doubt Radha was daughter of respective person so some teachers had responsibility to bring her good marks. It was not good. And Radha was not too duffer to pass the exam. But still nobody wanted to leave opportunity make her father happy because nobody can say when this person will help them in their problem.

Result was quite good and satisfactory to everyone. Raghav was passed with first class. But Radha stood first in the school. No need to say how. All his friends also passed pout the exam. Everybody was asking only marks. But was not interested to listen their marks. Now he had planned to take more education and it was not easy to him or his family. A poor farmer can't afford higher education but Bairagi sir convinced his parent to let him take more education. Raghu was ready taken any effort for education because he got inspiration from his teachers.

Radha went to her maternal uncle's village while Raghav started working with his family like for the cultivation the farm. Raghav could understand the value of parent's task for him therefore he was thinking about his parent and wanted to do something which will be make them proud one day.

Raghav took admission in junior college in the city because there village had only high school. For next class they had to go in city. Raghav was not feeling good there. Because in village there was some discipline and restrictions but here all were roaming like stray cattle. When he saw teacher he remember Rama kaka who was grazing his animals same way. And most important there was not Radha now in front of him. He wanted to focus on the lectures but could not. All friends knew the problem. Here they all were seating on the last benches as poor cows. He got the news that Radha took admission another city. And that also made him nervous about.

One day miracle had happened when he came on bus stand for college all friends came to him and shouted loudly that Radha is came back to here and took admission in our college. It was happiest moment that time for him, now started looking at her. Now he started taking an interest in classroom.

One day Raghav and his friends were taking tea with his friends where some boys were talking about Radha in wrong way. Raghav couldn't bear it, he wanted to beat them but Shyam stopped him to do so. All had made plan without knowing to Raghav. Whatever will happen they will always stood for each other. Same day, Radha was standing in the gallery with her friends. Raghav and his friends also were standing on the same gallery. One boy came to her whose character was well known to Radha. He proposed Radha that he likes her and he loves her. Radha didn't expect this. She started crying. This was then uncontrollable to Raghav

Nobody could understand what happened. All students started to run in the gallery. Raghu had bitten the boy very badly. Suddenly fight started again in group of both boys. Everybody was shock. Principal and Teachers came their and then problem solve. Principal called Raghav and Radha and that boy. Principal rusticated both for ten days.

Radha could not understand about Raghu why he was so hyper while it was her problem and she knew how to solve that. Next day she met Kanhayya to discuss the matter.

"What is your friend's problem? Why did he fight for me?"

"Means you don't know still why he fought for you. Ok then listen Radha he loves you a lot and not from yesterday but since he saw you first time in the school in 5th standard then tell me how could he bear this all."

Radha could not understand what to say. She dint know whom she was like, is also like her. She got great shock. Now how could she tell anyone why she took admission in this college only? She could not sleep at night even due this all condition. Both happiness and fear she felt first time in her life.

It was difficult to pass ten days for Raghu and now Radha too because after that everyone started talking to Radha with respect and nobody dared to look at her in wrong way. After her long waiting Radha saw Raghav. But now Raghav could see in her eyes. She thought he will come to me and talk. But still the recess he hasn't seen her at glance. She got angry and came to Raghav. Without any thinking she slapped Raghav. All were shock what happened but Raghav haven't any expression on his face but wanted to listen what she wanted to talk.

"I was thinking that you are so clever but you are most stupid boy. You are coward. How much you are selfish. At least think about others mind what they are suffering and you stupid if you love someone then dare to tell her or don't love to anyone." Radha told him something unexpected to Raghav.

All were shocked when she gave beautiful smile to Raghav and went away. All started shouting because at least she came to know about his mind. Indirectly she proposed him and Raghav got it. Instantly Raghav ran behind the Radha and caught her hand. Radha expected this

"Radha I am sorry. I could not tell because I had fear to loss you so. But I can't stop now. I love you Radha. And forever I will you."

"I love you too. By the way thanks to that stupid boy who proposed me and I came to know this. "She hugged Raghav.

Radha and Raghav started roaming together and hence it was problematic for someone. They both love each other, without any profit or loss. There love story started flourish in time. They lived much happy moment with each other. There were no mobiles and phones so no contact to each other only letter writing was the way. They started meeting in the temple, school, and college and so on. They promised each other that they will make their career and marry. Radha promised him that she never lives him and she will wait for him, even for whole life. But fortune had not willed that. It had something in its mind.

One Raghu was taking dinner with is parent and suddenly Sampat came in their house. Without asking anything he started beating him. Raghav couldn't understand what to do. He could also give reply but he controlled on himself. He told everything to Raghav's parents. His parents couldn't understand what to do to. Crowd gathered in front of his village and they started discussing about anything. Samapat gave warning to Raghav and his family but how could he satisfied with this only.

Early in the morning peon came to Raghu's home and told them to attend the Panchayat meeting. All went there and shocked to listen all the charges on Raghav. He knew that Radha haven't any mistake in this. She was seated only in the corner. Only she looked at Raghav as if she was telling that she wasn't responsible for anything there. And he should save her. Raghav accepted everything what charges on him by her father because he doesn't wanted to make her famous. To keep her innocent, he made himself criminal, he accepted all charges. Panchayat decided to either he should leave the village forever or his family leave the village but he chose option. And sign in the paper that he will never come back in the village.

How unfortunate it was. Radha met him secretly and said sorry for everything. And she promised him that she will wait for him forever. She promised that she will marry with him only, not to anyone.

And next day he left the village forever for the sake of his family; even at the time of his sister's marriage he was not informed. He felt very sad and did hard work. During these ten years he learnt so many things and efforts to prove himself. But today he was invited by the same people after many efforts. In fact it was victory of his love....

"Raghav Sir, Is it your village? Please call and asked someone to tress us" Mahesh words brought him in the present. Really is his village but how much it change. School is having new building, new garden. Everything is new; only that old principal office, old well and that tamarind tree.

"Mahesh move inside, this is the school. I can't believe that everything is change dude."

But Raghav is thinking about Radha how is looking after ten years. He just started imagine. But he believed that she would come there to see him. People started gathered around him. Happily they welcomed him. He saw his entire teachers but specially Bairagi sir, white hair, big spectacle on eyes but there was no need to search the sir. He directly went to him and saluted him by touching his legs. That the same respect he has shown to also. He met to his friends by hugging them without showing any formality. He took Bairagi sir with him one the stage. He could not believe on his eyes if it is the same village which expelled him out. But today he won everything and nobody will stop him to take his Radha from here.

He started his speech when he invited to guidance for the student. Actually till the date no any big guest came in the village. Almost whole village came to see him.

"Good morning friends. Today, it's very precious day for me. Because you can't feel this until you face this. I will guide because these teachers are great guide, I just want tell you my story. I can't tell you how much I am happy today. You it is not short period, ten years, I left everything. When I left the village I had nothing to do. I wanted to destroy my life. Nothing was left. Nobody had thought where this boy will go. I went to committed suicide but my friends came to me. They saved my life. I am here because of my friends and my love. To you can see this shining lamp but provided fuel is my friends and lightening lamp thread is my love.

You must keep and be such friend who always stays with you because this is most important property for your life. My friends did everything for my education even they left education. Even my friends gave money for my inn, exam fees, and hostel. I don't know how they manage d that but I can't forget them. I really thankful to you all to calling me here and fulfilled my desires to see my house once again. Best luck to you all for exam. Thank you."

He finished his speech and sat down. After finishing the programme he seated with his friends. Suddenly, Sampat came to him and Raghav gave him chair to seat. Raghav couldn't understand what to talk with him. But his eyes were saying everything; Raghav could see the repentance in his eyes.

"Raghav , I am sorry. I was wrong. I really misunderstood you. Please forgive me."

"Uncle what are doing? I don't have any complaint about please try to understand. In fact it was good for me. By the way where is Radha? I want to meet her." Raghav couldn't control but now he is not afraid.

"Come. ... We will go to home then will talk." Sampat told him.

Raghav and Sampat sat in the car and Mahesh started following the instructions gave bye him. How was Sampat, angry, fighter, had lot of proud. Now old and so sober, White hair, wick body. They reach to the home. Raghav became so happy for see his love. But something was there which was not expected to Raghav. Suddenly Raghav fallen down on the floor other people tried to catch him. Some they took Raghav on the bed. May be Sampat came to know the reason. Raghav saw the photo of Radha with garland. He could not believe on his eyes how it possible.

"Raghav, our Radha left us here a lot. I know what are you feeling but can you imagine my pain as father. You know I was responsible for this all. She was suffered from cancer. And I could not save her. You know she always asked me 'what will you say when Raghav will come and ask about?' she believed that one day you will come. Take this. She gave me for this and warn to give you in her last days." Sampat was talking all these things but Raghav was just looking at his face. He took this latter and open.

"Dear Raghav,

I know you are sad because when you will read this latter, I will not live in this world. You have many complaints about me. Don't think that I don't love you. I am really sorry. I was the responsible you problem. I came to know very early that you like. You know I just wanted to tell on the day of farewell. I also liked you from my 7th standard. I know you love me a lot but I didn't express it more. You went and my life deceived myself. I don't deceive you dear. I know many times we blame to woman for disloyalty. But I am always loyal to you. Please forgive me. I could not complete my promise. But remember I am always with you. I really wanted to live with you. But may be out fate don't want it whenever you will call mi I will come to you. I believe that one day you will come back to meet me. Take care.

Only your's Radha"

Raghav could not understand what to do. His eyes were full tears. Some tears fallen down on the letter due to that some letters were erased. He could not believe on his eyes Radha was standing in the corner, looking at him with smile.

***

10

Thread

Hi friends. How are you? What ...I... I am not fine. You know life plays a game sometimes that we forget our existence. And after that we just think about what game it played with us. It is not in our hand what we will get and when until life decides itself. Sometime we enjoy the living but sometimes the same life becomes boring and dwarf. Where we can see only darkness, no any way we get to get out from. And in this situation we suffocate very hardly. It's very difficult to want in this dark when are alone. In such situation someone is to be or not it makes great effect on us. That's very important to walk on this rout. Yes, we can easily walk on such ways, in such circumstances if we have the company.

My life is also the same journey where I am walking alone, and it is impossible to come back. I forgot to tell you about myself, please don't mind. Even much time I forgot myself. My name is Rajendra Deshmukh. But please don't think about my name. I am working in the automobile company in Gujarat. Unwillingly I came here. I didn't want to leave my home. After all you know that own house is so much important in the life. But I can't forget that moment when I came here with lot of suffering. Even when I came here, I hadn't had money in my hand. And nobody was there who could help me.

Come; let me tell you my story. I don't want to tell anyone but today I got chance to tell you this. I was living in small village in Maharashtra with my family. Today also they are living there only. My brother, sisters and parent are living there. I love my family so much and my life is incomplete without them. It's very important for me. They also love me a lot. I know that they also didn't feel happy when I left my house. But I was criminal in their opinion. They were right but where was I wrong in my point. They decided for them but I was right on my place. How can I tell them that love is everything? I did love and that is my mistake. But is it wrong to do the love.

I was very shying boy from my childhood. Even I was very shying to talk with the girls even. But when I saw her I really wanted to talk with her. But time I was not thinking about love or something, that you are thinking like. I was standing in the bank to fill the admission form. Suddenly somebody requested to fill her form. Hemangi first time I came to know her name. If she didn't come to me for fill up the form then I could not get her name even. I came to know her name that day. She was so beautiful and attractive. And her smile was so good.

She had taken the admission in the same class. That time I didn't know anything about her. But next day I came to know that she came in our village and so I was again happy. Just my mind was happy to talk with her. I felt something that I had never felt it before. What was that feeling? Any way. But from that we became friends. Even her aunty also said me to keep watch on her. Then we both started talking with each other and that sense I was very good for them all.

Same subject she selected as I took so we always started going together in each class. How much matured she was! She had always solution in any problem. When she was talking with me I was just looking in her eyes but she never opposed mi. May she could understand what I had in my mind but how can one girl say this to the boy. Many times she was crying whenever I saw her alone seated. She was always telling me that she got the chance for education then she must use the opportunity. Off course she was right. Therefore I could not tell her anything.

Now I understood that another relation can also be there between girl and boy instead love only. But our partial view cross here and force us to think unnecessary things. And that human mind. Slowly I turn my love into her friendship. And she was happy with me that I didn't do any wrong with her. I was telling everything her related with my life. And I was not hiding anything to her. She was my most faithful friend. And most important is that she was not telling to anyone. She was giving me suggestion also in correct manner.

I tried myself to control and make happy

with her friendship. But my mind was telling me that somewhere she was also thinking the same thing for me also. But I had fear about her anger and if suppose she is not thinking about me what I am thinking for her then? What to do. One day I decided to tell her everything about my love. I was prepared myself very perfectly. But I had no experience, what to tell her? And how did? There were many questions in my mind. First I decide that whatever she will reply I must accept. There was no possibility to tell anyone. And I couldn't take the help from anyone because it wasn't the social work to do together. From I was thinking what I should talk with her. My love was pure and true. And when you do anything with good mind then you will get potential. I had also got it.

I was waiting on the bus stand for her. I left three buses during the period and I knew that how it was difficult to get bus in those days. Hardly had we get one bus during two hours and up to that we had to wait. You can't imagine how speedily my wad beating when I saw her on the way. I thanked to the god whether I knew she would come. But that waiting was very important that day.

She greeted me with good morning but I was thinking what to say? She asked me three four times about my mood but what could I tell her? Somehow I came to college. But whenever I thought to tell her my heart started beating very fast. Finally with full of strength I stopped her out of the library and said her everything what is in my mind.

"Hemangi, I want to tell you something important. Please don't misunderstand about me. Just I want to tell you what I have in my mind for you. I don't know whether it is right out wrong, virtue or sin.

I really like you so much. I love you so much. I really felt something about you what I hadn't felt before that about anyone. Still today I didn't tell anyone this and may be never tell in future also. And I don't want to trouble you. I know we are good friends and may be it will affect. But I couldn't suppress my love, sorry. I will wait for your answer." With full of fear I left the place and ran away to canteen. It was horrible moment for me. I hadn't done this before. Somehow, I was just recovering myself; soon I got another shock to see Hemangi in front of me. She was looking at me but there weren't any feeling of love or anger. She sat slowly in front of me. I was complete blank in front of her. In fact what could I say?

"How is our life? When we want to laugh then we can't. I assumed that one day you would say me this. But still I was silent. In fact, no one is so happy than you when you come to know that someone loves you. You know this feeling is so awesome. But when you want to eat something and you are restricted for food, is most dangerous and hard to survive.

You like me its ok but I don't want to keep you in dark. Before loving me you must know my reality. Two years before my family did my marriage against of my desire. What could I do that time? Actually I wanted to take education. But my family hasn't well economic condition and they did my marriage. But my fate refused it. My husband was so drunkard and he is no more today but he made me widow. They all determined mi as unlucky for the family: Even my parent also. And there for my aunty took me here and started my education. She hasn't child. Now tell me how can I love? Still do you want to love me?"

"I didn't know about you before that but knew you. I don't love on your beauty but on you only. I will accept you in any situation. Now, after listening this, my love for you is more enriched my dear."

She went without any word. I could not get what wanted to tell because that much knowledge hadn't. But next day, when she came before me and smile with ecstasy, It was green signal for me. I was so happy and delighted. After that we are accepted each other. And near about three years we were in relationship, during that her family was also started talking with her because they wanted to do her second marriage. And here wanted to build our own nest.

Finally the day came. We both completed graduation. And my family had come to know about our matter. I told them that I wanted to marry with her. But they rejected her because she was widow and from different caste. That time I had two options either to choose her or my family. I wanted to take both because both were very important for me.

I don't know, either I was wrong or correct but I chose Hemangi. There is no specific reason that I can give with logical idea. I had to leave my village after her choice. I told her everything what happened at home. But she couldn't give me answer. She was confused about what to do. But finally after lot thinking she agreed.

We planned to elope from the village and I had some savings with me as well as I talked with my friend about this. He also was ready. And what then we left village with great secrecy. It was very difficult for us. But we dared because I got my real love.

We came in Ahmadabad to live where I got good job and I started. One my friend helped lot. He gave me so much help. She also wanted to live with me. We both were very happy with each other. She was very happy with me. But we both had one pain of family losing. They couldn't understand our love. I know it was against of them and their so called culture.

We were really happy with each other and started our new life. But my fate hadn't granted it. She was pregnant and that was very happy thing for me. What great news was for me! I can't tell you. We went to check up to the doctor and got happy news about my son. Now I was taking so much care for her. I always wanted to complete her each wish. We hoped that will to the village to meet both families. And when they will see their grandson they will forget everything. I planned everything.

One evening when I was working in the office one fellow came to bring me. He directly took me in the maternity hospital. I could not understand what was happened? Nobody was telling me really what had happened. I came to know that it Hemangi, who is in the hospital but I could not guess what was exactly happened? After some time doctor came to ask about me. They took in the cabin and said me that my wife had an accident and her condition was so critical. And it was very difficult to save her. Because due to pregnancy she had internal bleeding and it wasn't possible then. I was shocked to listen. I could not understand what to do. I requested doctors to save her anyhow. But everything was useless. They could not save her. She left me here with incomplete love. In fact I also wanted to die with her. But she left the symbol of our love- Hemraj. He is the symbol of our love and therefore I am living for him.

She didn't left me alone she left her eyes on me. In fact she is in my heart. She is always alive in my heart till is beating. She is always with me. Whether our love could complete life but it completed my life and I will live with her all memories.

      Now my Hemraj is in five standards. Many told me to do the second marriage but didn't take chance for him. We both are living very happily together. He wants to be the doctor. You know why? Because another Hemraj should not loss their mother and Rajendra should not loss there love one? He knows how much i love his mother. He likes to listens the stories of his mother. She is the most common thread between us. Without this one single thread we can't live. You know love is one thread which ties up people in one beautiful garland. I miss you Hemangi."

***